FREE FALL
and
HOME FIRE INFERNO
(Burn, Baby, Burn!)

Two Troubleshooters Stories

Suzanne Brockmann

Suzanne Brockmann Books
www.SuzanneBrockmann.com

Dedication

For the men, women, and children
who also serve by
keeping the home fires burning.

FREE FALL

Timeline:

This Troubleshooters story takes place
in early January 2010,
eight-ish months after *Breaking the Rules,*
and around two weeks before *Home Fire Inferno.*

CHAPTER ONE

"Shit."

Tony Vlachic's voice came through the radio headset loud and clear, right as Izzy hopped and popped.

Shit was right. The force of their chutes opening was intense—they were all gonna feel it for days—and Tony V wasn't the only SEAL giving voice to his pain. Izzy chimed in with a little inadvertent *Holy what the fuck* falsetto descant of his own, even as Markie-Mark Jenkins gave forth with a sternly worded reprimand to his sweet baby Jesus. Meanwhile, the FNG, Ferd McTurd—not his real name, but it would do until the youngster had earned the team's respect—laughed his crazy ass off.

"Let's at least *try* to pretend it's the dead of night," their LT and CO "Big Mac" MacInnough said mildly.

"Radio silence," their newly minted chief, Jay Lopez, ordered and all complaining stopped.

It seemed pretty pointless to play at stealth when the sun was shining with all its might. Still, it wasn't all *that* hard to shut-the-fuck-up, considering the awe-inspiring splendor of the scenery.

Up here, the world was a pretty freaking beautiful place.

The sky was crystal clear over the desert, but not too many miles away, well before the curving horizon, there was a full array of picture-perfect clouds stretching as far as the eye could see. And up here, Izzy could see pretty freaking far.

Beneath him, his fellow SEALs' open parachutes stacked in formation, one atop the other. Mark Jenkins had jumped first and was on point, with Tony V just after him, then Jay Lopez—the chief, gonna take some time to get used to *that*—then young Ferd, then Big Mac, then Izzy's SEAL-in-law Danny Gillman, then finally Izzy himself, last out of the plane and still at the highest altitude.

Of course, they were currently *all* at such a high fricking altitude, the few hundred feet between them didn't mean squat.

This was a HAHO jump—high altitude, high opening. They'd hopped out of a rather swiftly moving aircraft and within seconds popped open their chutes. The force of doing that was always teeth jarring.

Long before Ferd had joined the team, when Izzy himself was the Fuckin' New Guy—just a wee tadpole fresh out of BUD/S— he'd heard a story about a SEAL who'd dislocated his jaw on a HAHO when his lines got tangled. *That* had to have sucked—dude had had to cut away *and* slam his own jaw back into place to be able to talk so he could tell his teammates WTF. Happily, the gentleman had survived. SEALs were good at that—in fact, honing their survival skillz was one of the reasons they regularly did training exercises like this one.

And that initial brain-shaking jolt was usually the worst of a HAHO. After that, it was all slow and peaceful and gentle, a seventy- to eighty-minute ride, just gliding silently down from thirty thousand feet to the waiting earth below.

Assuming, of course, that enemy troops weren't also waiting for them to come within deadly rifle range. Which was why HAHOs were usually done in the dead of night at oh-dark-thirty, when the SEALs and their chutes would be invisible as well as silent.

Today's training op had been originally scheduled to include the covering pitch of black, but their flight had been delayed, and then delayed some more. Lieutenant MacInnough eventually had decided to jump despite the fact that the sun was already up. Izzy wasn't sure if that was because the BigMacster loved jumping or hated it.

Either way, here they were, flying through the bright blue morning sky.

Up! In the at! Mosphere! Up! Where the air is clear...

It was funny how the words to the old Mary Poppins song always came into Izzy's head whenever he HAHOed. In truth, the air up here at thirty-K feet was *so* clear, i.e. thin, that the SEALs needed oxygen to survive. They not only pre-breathed pure O2 for thirty minutes while up in the plane, but they jumped with masks and tanks in place.

The math that went into a jump like this was intense. The team leaders and aerospace physiology techs didn't merely calculate the altitude and timing for when to jump and when to deploy chutes. Numbers were also needed to make sure the team had enough oxygen to keep them breathing until they got down to a thicker part of the at! Mosphere!

But the techs also weighed each SEAL and each necessary piece of equipment that the SEALs would be strapping to their backs, and they distributed said necessary equipment among each team member so that they would all weigh close to the same amount after their chutes opened. This was done so that they all floated to earth at the same precise rate. It meant that the smaller guys like Jenkins were carrying a shit-load, while the bigger guys like the LT—the nickname *Big Mac* had been given to him with exactly zero irony—jumped with barely more than phone, dive-watch, and weapon.

"You... guys." That was Tony V again, breaking radio silence. "Do you *see* that... um..." His voice trailed off. "Uh-oh..."

He sounded strange—a little slurred and whole lot of weak, like the SEAL was full-on drunk after forty-eight hours of chugging jello shots.

Except just before they'd boarded the plane for this training mission, Tony had been super-lucid while giving Markie Jenkins and Danny-Danny-bo-banny a glowing report about the extremely awesome trip he and his fiancé had made up north to Seattle for some hipster indie film festival. Even though it had rained the entire time, they'd been put up at some fancy B&B and treated like movie stars.

Lots of grilled wild halibut and sleeping late with the sound of the rain against the roof. Tony had been out to his teammates for years now, so he didn't hesitate to tell when they'd asked—thank God DADT was finally on the verge of ending—adding that seeing Adam's latest film on the big screen was also pretty great, of course.

But here and now, as Izzy looked down, he saw that one of the canopies was meandering drunkenly off course, to the south. It was Tony. And Izzy knew instantly that his teammate was in some fucking serious trouble.

T's oxygen access was malfunctioning—had to be—and up here pulling off his mask wouldn't help. With their chutes deployed, it would take maybe twenty minutes—shit, maybe even more—to float down to an altitude where they could breathe without aid.

"Hypoxia!" Izzy said it aloud even as Tony self-diagnosed his own problem. Only what he said came out "Pox... See... Uh... *Fuck me.*"

Fuck me, indeed.

"Vlachic, cut away! Now!" Izzy said it at the same time that Chief Lopez did. MacInnough gave the exact same order.

"I'm going," Izzy announced to both men, not waiting for the order before he veered sharply south so that he could cut away, too. Because he was at the top of the stack, it made sense for him to be the one to go. He'd have the best shot at helping Tony. He popped his chute free and released himself from the harness.

And just like that, Izzy was back to heady free fall, zooming past his teammates, with only his reserve chute—packed correctly, please Jenkins's baby Jesus—to keep him from becoming a stain on the glaringly bright desert below.

In that instant, Izzy thought briefly of his wife, Eden—God, he loved her with his heart, with his soul, with every cell in his being— and of Tony's partner, Adam, who was just as thoroughly cherished.

Then he focused only on Tony, praying his teammate would find the strength to cut himself away. And Izzy tucked in his arms and turned his body into a rocket that would allow him to reach the other SEAL before it was too late.

If Tony didn't cut away...

Izzy would have one and only one chance to grab Tony as he hurtled past.

Please Gods, don't let him miss.

CHAPTER TWO

When Ben Gillman punched Wade O'Keefe in the face, he heard an echo of his older sister Eden's voice.

No drama, please, while Jenn and I are away.

Eden had said those very words to Ben yesterday, before getting into the cab that took her and their brother Danny's wife to the San Diego airport. The two women were flying to San Francisco, and then driving up to Napa for a wedding shower for one of Jenn's best friends. Eden went along because Jenn was pregnant and Danny couldn't go with her. His SEAL team was in deploy-any-minute mode.

Sixteen-year-old Ben had only been living in southern California with his brother and Jenn, *and* with his sister Eden and *her* Navy SEAL husband, Izzy—bouncing between their two equally awesome apartments—for just over seven months, but even in that short amount of time, he'd learned that deploy-any-minute mode *also* meant dialing back the drama to a negative five.

But here in the high school corridor, the drama-knob had been cranked to a hot eleven. The world had gone into a kind of weird slow-mo, with Wade staggering backwards as blood erupted out of his nose—an apt visual to the sharp explosion of pain in Ben's hand.

Holy crap, punching someone in the face hurt!

It was entirely possible Ben had broken his hand.

Wade hit the lockers with a rattling bang as two of the three kids he'd been torturing skittered away, booking it down the hall. Ironically, it was the slightest of the three, Ryan Spencer, who stayed. Ryan now shifted his weight back and forth as he attempted to stand shoulder to shoulder with Ben. He even put up his dukes like an old-school boxer—assuming boxing had an "elf" weight.

The kid was adorable with his sweet face and big blue eyes behind vaguely Harry Potter-esque glasses. Fucking Wade had been targeting Ryan for weeks with all kinds of asshole-ish behavior—from name-calling and taunting slurs to knocking into him in the hall.

Today's assault was one of full-on intimidation, with Wade blocking the exit to the boy's bathroom—keeping Ryan and his friends from leaving and getting to class on time. Ben had rounded the corner and seen the upperclassman's aggressive body language along with Ryan's stiff shoulders and courageously lifted chin, and something in him had snapped.

No one hassled Ben like that anymore—at least not here at his new high school. Sure, he still got whispers and stares—but that could be for any number of things. He was the new kid, he was diabetic, plus ever since he'd gotten his hair cut he was a ginger again, *and* he frequently got dropped off in the morning by a variety of camo-clad Navy SEALs. So the murmurs and looks weren't necessarily because he was gay. But some of them probably were— the world also being home to people who still clung desperately to ignorance and fear, like Wade O'Keefe, asshole jock.

But Wade had carefully kept his distance from Ben—probably because Ben's latest growth spurt had taken him into six-three territory. Yeah, he was still too skinny, but living with Danny and Izzy had inspired him to work out, and under their guidance, his hard work was starting to show. And, of course, Wade had probably made note of the whole dropped-off-at-school-by-SEALs thing.

Bullies targeted kids who were unlikely to fight back.

But it hadn't been that long ago that Ben had been in Ryan's shoes. And it had sucked. Especially when the other kids pretended not to notice the ongoing abuse. They were fearful—for good reason—of becoming the bully's next target.

But Wade didn't scare Ben.

And enough was enough.

"Hey, Wade," Ben had said, heavy on the faux-friendly as he'd approached all four boys. "Either ask Ryan to the prom, already, or *back* the fuck *off.*"

As the words were leaving his lips, he could imagine his sister's heavy sigh. *Drama-free* meant *not* taunting the homophobe with implications that *he* was also gay. Yeah, Ben got that. Although truth be told, Wade pinged Ben's gaydar far more even than adorbs little Ryan did.

Of course, Wade now immediately got defensive, and Ben just tuned out the football player's fugly *faggot*-filled word-vomit, instead rolling his eyes and laughing as he looked at Ryan and his two equally wide-eyed friends.

It *may* have been the laughing that pushed Wade over the edge.

Or maybe it was Ben moving in closer, because he knew that would make Wade take a step back—which would give Ryan and co an opportunity to get out of the bathroom and run for cover.

But instead, Wade shoved Ben, both hands against his chest.

"Ah, so it's *me* you want to dance with," Ben said as he held up his arms in a graceful waltz position, even while imaginary Eden face-palmed from her perch on his shoulder. His sister could face-palm like no one else on the planet. Of course, it didn't help that Ben could hear Izzy, over on his other shoulder, laughing his ass off.

And yup. *That* was when Wade swung at him.

It was less of a punch and more of a wild flail. Wade sent his arm roughly in Ben's direction, and yeah, there was a clenched fist at the end of it. But it was slow and ugly—in fact, it looked exactly the way both Izzy and Dan had described it, when each had given Ben their personal version of a crash course in self-defense. Idiots and/or douchebags who lost their temper and erupted in violence tended to be careless amateurs when it came to fighting—both SEALs had told Ben that.

Ben blocked the flail easily with his left hand, pushing Wade's arm to the side and causing the heavier boy to lose his balance and stumble. Thank you, Izzy and Danny.

But it was too early to take a final bow.

With a roar, Wade came back around, this time attempting to grab Ben in a bear hug and knock him down to the ground. But again, his charge was fueled by anger—a mindless, blind rush that Ben easily sidestepped.

It was, however, time to run because Wade had at least fifty pounds on Ben, if not more. And now it was Danny and Izzy's friend Mark Jenkins's voice that rang in Ben's head. Mark was what Izzy called *height challenged*—a lean, compact, quick-footed SEAL with freckles and hair that was not quite as vibrantly red as Ben's, but close.

When you're up against a bigger guy, Mark had told Ben, *never let him get too close.*

If Wade *did* knock Ben down, someone was going to get badly hurt. But Ryan and his friends were still frozen in the doorway of the boy's bathroom, and there was no way Ben was going to run away and leave them there.

Unless he was absolutely sure Wade was chasing *him*.

But before he could dance away, using his body language to taunt the heavier boy into following, Wade came at him again.

Only this time, as Ben moved to sidestep the lunge, he slipped. His foot skidded, just a little bit.

Just enough to slow him down.

He recovered and didn't hit the floor, but Wade got close enough to grab his T-shirt with one ham-sized hand. Wade used his other arm like a cudgel, and—*wham!*—whaled Ben in the side of his face. The blow ricocheted his head into the concrete block wall next to the boy's room. He hit with a sick-sounding thud—it was hard enough so that he saw actual stars.

No tweeting birds, though. But stars were definitely twinkling.

And so okay, now *death* was a possibility, up there along with an ass-kicking, and as Ben felt Wade raining even more blows on him, he ducked, arms over his head, so the other boy's giant fists hit his back.

If you do get trapped, Mark Jenkins had stressed, *don't try to pull away, you'll never get free. Step toward your adversary—he won't expect that.*

Or throw up on him. Eden's advice. *That always works.*

That *was* a serious possibility. His stomach was heaving, his head was throbbing as Ben turned back toward Wade and moved toward him, straightening up into a full-on embrace. And yup, Wade *wasn't* expecting that. Not only did Ben get a surprise greeting from Wade's giant-ass boner—*What?*—but he also caught a break as the bigger boy couldn't keep hitting him, at least not as effectively, from that face-to-face proximity.

Up this close, Ben also noted that Wade had really nice skin—smooth and blemish-free surrounding a pretty mouth. But he also had a serious case of dog-ass breath. Holy crap, that was deadly. Ben had to hold his nose. For a half a second, time froze as Wade stared back into Ben's eyes.

And for the weirdest nano-second, Ben thought that maybe Wade was going to kiss him.

Don't hesitate.

Those instructions came in a full variety of voices. Izzy's. Dan's. Mark's. Eden's. Even Jenni, who usually preached non-violence.

So Ben didn't wait to see what Wade was going to do next—be it kiss or death-delivering chokehold. He stepped even closer and brought his leg between Wade's. He may have been skinny, but the muscles in his thighs were solid and strong, and it didn't take much to swing his right leg up and completely crush Wade's balls.

Wade screamed as he let Ben go, but he was clearly fucking insane, because even though Ben danced back, Wade lunged at him again. And that was when Ben popped him with a hard, carefully placed right jab to the nose.

Ow.

The force sent Wade slamming noisily into the lockers, Ryan's friends scattered, but Ryan stayed. God, he was cute, but then again, Ben had always been a little bit in love with Harry Potter.

"Go," Ben told Ryan as Wade sank down onto the floor across the hall, clutching both his balls and his face as he moaned in pain. "Now. Before a teacher shows up. No point in you getting suspended, too."

But Ryan hesitated. "My mom's a doctor," he said, "so I know some stuff and—your head hit the wall really hard. You need to tell someone and get that checked. Promise me, Ben."

Ryan Spencer knew his name. Huh. "I will, I promise. Thanks. But *go,*" Ben said again, and the younger boy finally dashed away.

And yup, clomping down the hall that led from the main office came a bevy (pride? gaggle? Ben was never sure which word applied) of teachers and administrators, including the portly security guard who sat near the front door, as well as the new vice principal, Ms. Quinbey, who was in charge of discipline. She was shaking her head in resigned disapproval as she approached.

"Mr. Gillman, I didn't expect to see you here," she told Ben. She was *maybe* Jenn's age, at most. She had to work it, hard, with the costume, hair, and make-up, to deliver the stern and scary.

Ben backed even farther away from Wade, holding his hands up in a gesture of surrender.

But it was Wade who spoke, playing the pity card. "He hit me!" He didn't bother attempting the *He hit me first* lie. He was well aware that that wouldn't play. However, it was very evident that *some*one had hit him, so...

Besides, it didn't really matter who threw the first punch—or in this case, the first shove. The school had a zero tolerance policy for fighting.

No doubt about it, Ben and Wade were both seriously screwed.

Somewhere up in Napa, Eden and Jenn were probably having a

leisurely breakfast with a group of Jenn's friends. Somewhere on the Coronado Navy base, Izzy and Dan were no doubt doing some kind of crazy crap to keep their SEAL super-powers functioning at their usual high levels.

As Ben was escorted to the front office, he also knew, without a doubt, that what he'd just done was going to seriously screw up *their* days, too.

CHAPTER THREE

Adam Wyndham's agent sent the news via email.

He didn't get the job.

Shit. The role was one that he wanted—badly. The script was well written and the movie was destined for the bigger film festivals—maybe even Sundance or SXSW.

But it was the character—intriguing, complex, a blur of both darkness and light—that had set Adam on fire.

He reached for his phone to text his fiancé, Tony, who always knew exactly what to say to soothe Adam's pain. Tony always put things into perspective using words like *disappointment* and *irritation* instead of *pain* and *anger*, or even *miffed* instead of bat-shit, forehead-vein-pulsing *outraged.*

Adam smiled just thinking about that. As an actor, he was drawn to both drama and hyperbole, taking what was, in fact, merely a disappointment, and ballooning it into soul-wrenching agony.

So he didn't get a role he wanted. Was he disappointed? Yes. Was he in agony? Nope.

Tony's even touch brought everything into a more realistic point of view, allowing Adam to recognize that his failure to get this job probably wasn't personal. The casting director didn't have some terrible vendetta against him. They'd no doubt gone with another actor who had a different look. Someone taller, probably. It happened.

Adam didn't need Tony to tell him that.

At the same time, Adam didn't need a reason to text Tony with a quick message: *Sitting here loving you madly.*

Tony didn't text him back—probably because he was running ten miles in his BDUs, boots, backpack and all, sweat pouring off of him…

And yeah, like *that* wasn't hot. Sometimes Tony came home already freshly showered, and sometimes he came home sticky and dirty, still in a sweaty uniform that needed to be peeled off.

Adam liked it both ways. Most of all, he liked days like today where he wasn't working, so he'd actually *be* here when Tony got home.

He shot his husband-to-be another quick text: *Chinese take-out later? Maybe MUCH later...? :-)*

And, yes. He'd become one of those guys who texted smiley faces to his partner. But so-the-fuck what. Sue him for being happy.

Because minor disappointments aside, today was going to be a really nice day.

Of course, that was when the house line rang.

CHAPTER FOUR

"Adam, oh good, you're there!" Eden looked across the hotel lobby to where Jenn was sitting with her friend Maria. She gave her sister-in-law a thumbs up and what she hoped was an *everything's a-okay* smile.

"I am," Adam said from his home on Coronado. He and Tony shared the sweetest little cottage not far from the island's charming downtown. Eden tried not to be envious of them—easy to do because they were both great guys, and it wasn't as if they didn't have their own challenges. While the repeal of *Don't Ask, Don't Tell* had just been signed into law by the President and everyone knew that change was coming, it hadn't happened yet. And although Tony was out to his friends and teammates, they all still had to tread carefully. "And you're... oh, wait, isn't this...?" He answered his own question. "The wedding shower long weekend. You're up in Napa with Jenn."

"Yes, I am," she said, no doubt sounding more grim than she'd intended. This trip was supposed to be fun, but it was exhausting hanging out with so many women she didn't know. They were all professionals, too. Lawyers, doctors, congresswomen even. And then... there was Eden, who'd busted her ass to get her GED, and who'd pulled in her biggest salary while stripping in Vegas.

"Is everything okay?" Adam asked with a wariness in his tone that broadcast his hope that she was not calling to ask a favor. "Is Jenn... ?"

"Jenn's fine," Eden said. At eight months pregnant, her brother Dan's wife glowed with such good health, it was obnoxious. But in a good way, she quickly corrected herself. "But—and I'm so sorry to have to ask you this, but I just got a call from Ben's school. He got into a fight and he's actually being suspended—"

"Oh, *shit*," Adam said, laughing his surprise. "Really?"

"Yes, really." Eden sighed heavily. "I was hoping it would be better here."

"Oh, God, it is," Adam told her, all reservation gone from his voice. "That wasn't *that* kind of *Oh, shit*, it was more of an *Even when it's better it's not perfect Oh, shit.* Honey, trust me, it's *so* much better for Ben at this school. I can tell just from talking to him—God, just from *looking* at him. He's doing *really* well. But there's always gonna be assholes, wherever he goes. That's just life in America. So *Oh, shit*, you know?"

"I guess so," she said.

"I know so. How can I help? You want me to go get him? Buy him an ice cream?"

"Yes, please." Eden closed her eyes. "But check his blood levels before the ice cream." Ben was diabetic, and being in a fight had probably messed up his blood sugar. "Thank you *so* much. I called the base and spoke to the senior chief, and both Izzy and Danny are doing some kind of training jump. Tony, too. And Mark and Chief Lopez. *Every*one's gone. They won't be back for... I don't even know how many hours."

"Oh, good," Adam said darkly. "A jump. Thanks for sharing. God, I hate jump days."

Eden did, too. The idea of Izzy leaping from a plane and falling to earth with only a piece of fabric to keep him from splattering on the hard ground below... "I shouldn't have told you," she said. "But..."

"You had to tell someone," Adam guessed, "and you didn't want to tell Jenn, because God forbid the anxiety makes that baby suddenly pop out of her—which is crazy-thinking, by the way? That baby's not coming out until it's good and ready. But whatever, and yay, *I* won the prize. Jump day. Whoo-hoo!" His laughter was a mix of admiration and disgust. "You and I are so much alike, it's scary."

"Maybe after you pick up Ben," Eden said, "you could, you know, swing past the base?"

"Casually drop by. It's already on my to-do list," Adam reported. "I'll text you when I know they're safely on the ground. And oh, yeah? As long as you're up in wine country, Toots, Tony likes a full-bodied Cabernet Sauvignon. And I like whatever Tony likes, so..."

"Got it," Eden said. "Thanks, Pookie. Glare at Ben for me."

"That you'll have to do yourself," he said, and then out-obnoxious-nicknamed her by dropping a "Later, Cupcake," before cutting the connection.

As Eden hung up, too, she could feel Jenn watching her, so she forced another smile and reported, "Adam's gonna get Ben."

And then she went and got herself another cup of coffee, because it was going to be a long, *long* morning.

CHAPTER FIVE

Izzy tried to slow his dive by opening up his arms and legs just before he nearly hit the edge of Tony's canopy.

This was not the right way to do this—get tangled in the para-fucking-chute and kill them both—but it was better than missing him.

Tony hadn't cut away—hypoxia's loss of oxygen to the brain could make the smartest men stupid—and Izzy grabbed on to anything he could—Tony, his pack, the lines—anything. Izzy clenched his entire body and clung like a motherfucker, refusing to let go, locking himself around his teammate with his arms and legs, wishing he wasn't wearing these gloves so he could grip with his fingertips, too, but knowing that even if he'd managed to pull them off during that dive, his hands would've frozen and been even more useless than they currently were.

The chute miraculously held, bouncing under his sudden additional weight, and then dropping—marginally—faster than the other six SEALs.

Tony's eyes were open, but no one was home. You'd think the jolt of suddenly being hit by a human bullet would've woken the guy up, but he'd completely checked into the stupor suite at the Hotel Hypoxia.

Izzy heard the chatter over his radio headset—the chief asking him for Tony's condition, and the CO already talking up the chain of command, requesting medical assistance on the ground.

Except they were jumping into the desert, which was, as the word implied, deserted. They were many miles from the base. Even if the Navy immediately sent a Blackhawk, Izzy and Tony were gonna hit the ground first.

"He's in trouble, boss," Izzy reported as he quickly fumbled some of his favorite short bungee cords free from his vest and hooked himself to Tony. He kept his legs locked around him, too, as he then checked the SEAL's mask and the tube leading to his oxygen bottle. Step one in troubleshooting was always to tap the mic and say *Is this thing on…?*

Everything was correctly attached, and the apparatus appeared to be working—except for the fact that Tony clearly wasn't getting enough O2. The malfunction might've been with the gear, or it might've been with Tony himself—couldn't count that out. Not yet, anyway.

Tick tock. Time was steadfastly marching forward the way time was wont to do, and there was only so long a human could exist without oxygen.

Izzy moved quickly to his plan B and unplugged Tony's hose from the O2 tank connector in his vest. "Might need a portable decompression chamber," he announced over his mic. "Or two. And a hospital corpsman on the ground would be nice." Hint, hint, Chief Lopez. "And maybe a coupla pizzas. I wouldn't say no to extra cheese."

"A decom*press*ion…?" he heard Big Mac echo, along with Chief Lopez's warning, "Zanella, what the hell…?" and Danny's "Zanella, are you fucking kidding me!"

They weren't stupid. They all knew exactly what he was going to do. It was what they would do, too, if they were here, clinging to Tony V. like a giant space monkey.

And now the conversation was temporarily over because Izzy was holding his breath after unfastening his own tube from his bottle's connector in his vest. He popped Tony's hose into his, hoping the other man was still capable of drawing air into his lungs by his lonesome.

But… Nothing. He got nothing from the T-man.

So he exhaled hard as he unfastened Tony's hose and reattached his own, drawing in a deep lungful of the good ol' O2 before popping both of their masks free.

Fuck it was cold, but death was even colder. He covered Tony's icy mouth and nose with his mouth and forced the damn oxygen into him. Izzy slapped his mask back onto his own face to draw another breath—rinsing and repeating one, two, three more times before Tony coughed and blinked and even retched a little.

And then—oh, good, because this wasn't hard enough—he began to struggle, trying to get away from Izzy.

There was something called the *oxygen paradox*, and it basically went like this: When treating hypoxia with oxygen, the symptoms sometimes got worse right before they got better. And although T was now breathing on his own, he was still badly disoriented. Also, he was wildly sucking in this thin-ass non-air, which wasn't helping the sitch.

Izzy knew a thing or two about fighting with a Navy SEAL, even a groggy and weak one. Bungee cords or not, it was only a matter of time before Tony wrenched his ass free, sending Izzy back into a sky-dive while Tony slowly floated back into hypoxia and certain death.

Arguing with him wasn't going to get it done. There was really only one way to guarantee Tony would make it to the ground still alive.

Izzy slapped the mask back onto Tony's face, connected T's tube to Izzy's tank, and then went for the three-ring release that would cut away Tony's chute and send them back into free fall.

Together.

It was a gamble—a big one—the assumption that breathing Izzy's O2 would bring Tony back to cognizance in enough time so he'd return the favor and not let Izzy die. But it was the only way they'd both survive, and Izzy was willing to take that risk.

As they plummeted to earth, with Izzy's legs still locked around Tony, as Tony still flailed and tried to shake him free, Izzy recognized his own telling signals of hypoxia as he breathed the frozen, too-thin not-quite-air.

The brilliant sky took on a haze of red, and Izzy could feel his heart accelerating as his mind sputtered and disconnected to a place where nothing hurt and nothing mattered because he simply didn't care. "Z... out," he managed to say, even as a part of him scoffed at the lameness of what could well be his final words before shuffling off this mortal coil.

Because he did. He cared. Truly, madly, deeply.

Eden. *Eden.* Izzy focused on the sound of his heartbeat racing in his ears, as his body attempted to find the oxygen he needed from somewhere, anywhere. Eden. *Eden.*

Way in the distance, tinny and metallic, a song played in his head.

Making love with you has left me peaceful, warm, and tired...

Okay, those lyrics weren't going to help him stay awake. Izzy fast-forwarded to the refrain and forced himself to loudly sing along.

CHAPTER SIX

The other kid was a little bit shorter than Ben, but was probably half again his weight.

Big guy. Broad shoulders, solidly built.

A football player.

Of course.

As Adam went into the high school office, both boys were slouched in hard plastic chairs that were part of a row lined up against the wall, in what was clearly the designated punishment zone. He'd sat in similar seats plenty of times during his own high school years, even though he'd dropped out when he was only sixteen. Seriously, the colors and even the smell—he'd caught the first whiff of that unique public school aroma right when he'd walked past the guard and into the building—were enough to trigger flashbacks.

With luck, he wouldn't have to be here for long.

Eden's little brother Ben and his fight-club adversary had left three of those ugly plastic seats empty, like a no man's land between them, as they both held medical icepacks against various body parts.

The football star was nursing both a bloody nose and his crotch, while Ben was icing the knuckles of his right hand and the side of his head.

Ben looked up as the door closed behind Adam, a defiant apology in his blue eyes. His face also held a hint of relief—probably that it was Adam who'd come instead of his brother Dan or Izzy. He knew that Adam's can of whoop-ass was considerably smaller for a whole slew of reasons.

The football player's focus remained on the industrial tile floor but his assholeishness wafted off of him in near visible waves. His casual indifference was almost laughably feigned. And Adam knew from his own past experience of having gotten the crap beaten out of him, that this kid was both frightened *and* mean. And considering the size difference between the two boys, it was a miracle that Ben wasn't in the hospital.

"Are you okay?" Adam asked.

"Yeah." Ben took the ice away from his head. "But there's a pretty big bump."

Adam leaned forward, thinking he would probably have to feel it, but there it was, visible to the naked eye. "Holy shit," he said. There was an egg, like something from a cartoon, just above Ben's ear.

The frosty-haired school receptionist glared in response to his language, and the football star himself even glanced up. His eyes widened in what Adam had come to recognize as home-team recognition.

And wasn't *that* a surprise.

Yeah, Adam may have been a movie star. But, no, as an out, gay actor, he'd mostly appeared in gay-themed indie films—with the exception of the more mainstream *American Hero*, the story of a gay soldier and the man he'd fallen in love with, set in war-torn Europe during World War Two.

Haters had publicly boycotted that film due to its alleged hot man-on-man action, AKA several very sweet and tender kisses, several slightly more passionate kisses, and several tastefully filmed, fade-to-black love scenes between Adam and the actor playing his true love.

But although that movie was still a critical favorite, it had been years since the firestorm fueled by its release.

So the football star *may* have seen Adam's photo on his local hate group's Facebook page, or—and the *or* was *way* more likely—this young man spent a significant amount of time locked in the privacy of his bedroom, streaming boy-meets-boy rom-coms and angsty coming-out dramas on his computer, and probably whacking off to the more intimate scenes.

As the boy refocused his gaze back on the floor, Adam took a longer look at him, because a bump like that hadn't just magically appeared on Ben's head. Whoever had put it there had had a serious boatload of intent to harm.

In a world that celebrated blond hair, blue eyes and a square jaw, this boy might've been called handsome, but there was something slightly... *off* about him.

Adam let himself stare openly, knowing from experience just how disconcerting that could be. And sure enough the kid glanced up at him again and...

Bingo—it was his eyes. The pale blue color didn't help, but it was the lack of life within that flattened them and made him seem cold and dead.

He was destined for greatness, provided his life's goal was to be a serial killer or the model for a Neo-Nazi recruitment poster.

But then Adam noticed the array of scars on the boy's face. One above his left eyebrow, one next to his nose, on his right cheek, on his chin, on his left cheek, too...

Just as Ben's bump hadn't gotten there on its own, those scars hadn't magically appeared, either.

Adam had gotten the mean part right, but he'd greatly underestimated the level and degree of this kid's well-grounded fear.

Jesus.

As the football player's gaze slithered back to the safety of the floor, Adam sat down next to Ben, who reported, "The nurse has been checking me regularly for a concussion. I'm not supposed to sleep—of course the minute she says that, I immediately need a nap."

"Don't they, like, take you to the hospital when you've had a head injury?" Adam asked.

"You got here pretty fast," Ben said.

"How about your blood sugar levels?" Ben's diabetes scared Adam more than any ass-kicking from a homophobe.

"I checked it while I was in the nurse's office," Ben reassured him. "I'm good. I had a little orange juice."

"Doesn't the fact that you had to have a little orange juice mean you're *not* good?" Adam countered.

"No, it just means it's a normal day," Ben said. "I check levels pretty regularly. It's not a big deal."

"So, are you, like, his boyfriend?" the football player spoke in a tone that was the very definition of a vocal sneer. It was so gloriously exact, Adam almost stopped and asked him to say it again so he could pay full attention and put it in his actor's toolbox. "That's disgusting. He's, like, fourteen, and you're, like, forty."

"Oh, I am *not* forty," Adam said indignantly. "FYI, he's sixteen and he's my Navy SEAL fiancé's teammates' brother—S apostrophe on that team-mates', *Junior*, because there are two of them related to Ben. And did I mention they were Navy SEALs? *Three* Navy SEALs, along with my fiancé, the *Navy. SEAL.*"

So much for being careful until DADT was over for good.

The football boy shifted as far as humanly possible from Adam, who inhaled deeply and then exhaled a long, cleansing breath before he looked at Ben and said, "I flashback to the horrors of my own high school days pretty fucking easily."

Ben coughed, and Adam looked up to find a woman standing directly in front of them. Her suit, hair, and make-up all screamed *Respect me!* Her shoes, however, announced her pathetically low public educator's salary. Oh, honey, no...

"I'm Ms. Quinbey, the vice principal. Are you Mr. Gillman?" she asked, her voice clipped with her implied disapproval of his F-bomb.

"No, I'm a family friend," Adam said, standing up, resisting the urge to alliterate further as he introduced himself. Quinbey was taller than he was, and she stood like a former ballerina, shoulders back, head high. "*Petty Officer* Gillman is currently out training with his SEAL team. As is Petty Officer Zanella, Ben's other legal guardian. Their wives, Jenn Gillman and Eden Zanella, are out of town. That's why they asked me to come."

The football boy laughed snarkishly at that, and when Adam glanced at him, the boy said, "At least I have *real* parents. Christ."

Dan, Jenn, Izzy and Eden had all worked liked hell to get Ben away from his abusive "real" parents, and Adam found himself looking at those scars again and wondering how many of them this boy's "real" father had caused. But that was neither here nor there.

"There should be a letter on file giving me permission to sign Ben out," Adam told the stern woman again, "or do whatever it is I have to do to take him to the hospital so he can get properly checked. Have you *seen* the bump on his head? It's not my place to make decisions about things like this, but I'm sure Ben and his family will be having a discussion about whether to press charges for assault."

Them was fightin' words, and the football player shifted uneasily at that.

But right on cue, as if he'd seen the good-cop-bad-cop script Adam was using, Ben spoke up. "No one's pressing charges," he said. "Adam, that's insane. Wade and I had an... um... a *disagreement* that... got out of hand."

"A disagreement?" Adam repeated. Of course Football's name was *Wade*. "About what?"

Ben hesitated, looking over at the football player who was now looking back at them with the tiniest spark of something in his otherwise dead eyes. It might've been hope, but it was probably just more fear.

"That's between Wade and me," Ben said. His voice was even but he was looking pointedly at Football while he said it. "It *was* between Wade and me. Very unmistakably between Wade. And me."

No doubt about it, Ben was talking in code to ol' Wade here. It didn't take much for Adam to guess exactly what had been "between" Wade and Ben as they'd fought. But even though Wade's face was turning red, Ms. Quinbey remained clueless, so Adam kept his face impassive, too.

But he couldn't wait to tell Eden. *Our little Ben was cool as ice while he blackmailed that bully motherfucker, right in front of the vice principal! I was so proud...*

"But I'm willing to just let it go and not talk about *any* of it," Ben continued, stressing that *any*. "Provided that, in the future, Wade keeps his distance from my friends and me. In return, I'll keep my distance from him. I'll never talk about him—in fact, I'll never even think about him again." He aimed his words at Wade. "Does that sound fair?"

Wade nodded almost jerkily, but Quinbey was not having it. "School policy requires at least one mediated meeting for the two of you, with our guidance counselor, before readmission."

"I don't have anything to say," Ben repeated. "But if we have to, we'll go to the meeting and even sing Kumbaya." He looked at Wade again. "You'll have to take the high harmony." Back to Quinbey. "But there's nothing to talk about. We've resolved our issue, and we're not going to fight again. Right, Wade?"

Wade found his voice, cleared his throat. "Right," he said, looking up at the vice principal. "Ma'am." But the look he then gave to Ben was not one of thanks.

The phrase *shooting daggers* sprang to mind.

But Ben's eyes were narrowed as he gazed back at Wade—this kid wasn't naive.

Adam stood up. "Well, *that* was fun. Time to take Ben to the hospital."

Ben stood, too, and Adam knew just from the way he moved that he was more badly bruised than he was letting on. Still, no point in letting Wade know that. Let him think Ben was made of Teflon, because in truth he was.

"Have one of Ben's guardians call me to discuss his return to school," Ms. Quinbey said.

"I suspect they'll want a meeting," Adam said. "Have you met them?"

"Not yet."

"Oh, you will," he told her.

Ben laughed, but then winced and then covered his wince with a smile. Odds were he'd cracked a rib.

Again, he was not willing to let Wade know that.

As Adam followed Ben to the door, Quinbey went back into her office with a quiet, "Let me know when Mr. O'Keefe's parents arrive," to the receptionist.

It was as he was going into the corridor, right after Quinbey's inner office door closed, that he heard Wade mutter, "Fucking faggots should all die."

Ben heard it, too.

As Adam closed the office door behind them, he looked at Ben and said, "Changing hearts and minds where e're we go. Tra la!"

Ben laughed. "He doesn't have to like me," he started.

"He just has to stay away from your *friends*," Adam said as they left the building and headed for his car, parked in one of the visitor's spots. "So who is he?"

Ben played dumb. "Who's who? What?"

"Yeah," Adam mocked him. "*What*? Can't bullshit a bullshitter, baby. You got into this fight with Wade because, why exactly? He was picking on someone, I don't know, shall we say... *special*?"

But Ben shook his head as he got into the passenger seat. "Wade was just picking on... someone. Yes, special, because we're all special, thanks. But the why is because I'm done pretending I don't notice."

"That's good," Adam said, starting his car. "Being done. But just be sure to watch your back, because Wade isn't done with you."

"Whatever." Ben fastened his seatbelt.

Adam backed out of the parking spot. "I'm serious, Ben. He's gonna come for you, although what he's gonna do when he gets you, I'm... not quite sure. I mean, *hello*!"

Ben met his eyes at that. "I told Wade I wouldn't talk about—"

"I know," Adam said. "And I respect that. But attraction is a weird thing, and at the risk of freaking you out—"

"Oh, my God," Ben said.

"I just want to say that if things got hot and heavy between you and Wade—"

"You're definitely freaking me out!"

Adam just spoke over him because this needed to be said, "—you wouldn't be the first person in this car to hook up with someone who tried to beat you up."

Ben was muttering something now that sounded like, "TMI, TMI, oh, please, please, don't..."

Adam squared his shoulders and kept going. "But I can honestly tell you that a guy like that is the polar opposite of good boyfriend material. He's not just a bad boy—he's dangerous. As in majorly fucked up. Take it from someone who knows."

"Can we please not talk about this?" Ben begged. "I mean, I appreciate your openness and honesty—I love you, I do, and I love Tony, too, but... Wade? No. No. Nope." He shook his head.

"I'm here if you need me," Adam said. "Tony is, too. I hope. Mind if we, um, go to the doctor on the base?"

"Uh oh," Ben said, clearly making note of that *I hope.* "Did the team deploy this morning?" The rest of his question, which was *And you wanna go to the base to attempt to find clues as to where they went* was silent.

"No," Adam countered. "It's not... It's just, you know, a training exercise." He glanced over to find Ben watching him expectantly, so he said it. "They're doing HAHO jumps today."

Ben swore pungently. "God, I wish I'd known before..."

"Helping a kid in desperate need of rescue?" Adam finished for him. "What, were you just going to walk away?"

"*Damn it,*" Ben said. "I hate HAHOs. Does Eden know?"

"Yep."

The kid put his face in his hands. "And I went and did this. *Shit!*"

"It's not that big a deal," Adam lied. "I mean, the team does 'em all the time. They're good at them. Which is a result of them doing them all the time, right? So it's a good thing. When they do the fucking HAHOs."

Ben looked up at him, eyebrows raised.

"I think Tony likes doing 'em," Adam explained his convoluted rationalization. "I mean, he pretends it's a pain in the ass, but..."

"Izzy likes them, too," Ben said. "Danny doesn't talk about it. I think he knows Jenn gets freaked out. Jay once told me he doesn't like 'em, because you have to restrict any diving—deep diving—a few days before going up in the plane, and he'd rather be diving."

"Out of all the SEALs I know, and I've met a lot of 'em," Adam said as he headed for the bridge to Coronado, "Jay Lopez is the only sane one."

CHAPTER SEVEN

Jay Lopez was no longer quite so certain about his promotion to chief.

And after this training op was over and he had a little time to spend reflecting, he was going to give the whole being-a-decision-maker thing his full attention.

Right now, as he cut away his parachute and tucked his head down into an extra aerodynamic free-fall dive, he could hear Izzy Zanella singing over his radio headset.

With Izzy, singing didn't necessarily mean he was feeling hypoxia's lack of oxygen, but in this case he probably was.

Jay hadn't been surprised when Izzy had given Tony access to his oxygen bottle. This wasn't the first time the big, gregarious SEAL risked his own life for a teammate.

Izzy had run into a hot zone to rescue Mark Jenkins, and gone into a sniper's kill zone to save Dan Gillman, who had been on the verge of bleeding out from a direct hit to his thigh. Izzy'd actually given Dan a battlefield infusion, literally opening a vein for him, hooking them together through IV tubing and then nearly dying himself when he gave away a little too much of his own blood.

Today, it was Tony's life that Izzy was saving. Tomorrow it was just as likely to be Jay or Lieutenant MacInnough, or Ferd the FNG. When Izzy was on your team, he absolutely had your back.

Right now, Izzy and Tony were tumbling as they, too, fell toward earth. The awkward randomness of their descent slowed them down a bit—just a bit—as Jay channeled his inner Rocketman and pulled his arms minutely closer to his body, in an attempt to increase his speed.

He was carrying his medical gear—that was good, at least. As was the fact that Izzy was still singing some ancient pop song. As long as he was singing, he was still alive.

Of course, that was the moment that Izzy fell silent.

"Stay with us, Iz," Jay said over his mic, wishing he had hands on the other man. He knew what to do to keep a teammate from bleeding out. He knew how to restart a heart, how to splint a near-catastrophic break. He could probably even deliver a baby in a pinch.

His training and skill as a hospital corpsman had undergone trial by fire, plenty of times. He had faith in his abilities.

But if he couldn't get to Izzy, he wouldn't be able to help the man.

But right now, Izzy wasn't alone. "Tony," Jay said, raising his voice. "Vlachic! Wake up!"

CHAPTER EIGHT

Tony's first thought was *Whoever this was, he wasn't Adam.*

It had been a long, *long* time since Tony had woken up with a big, heavy stranger wrapped around him, and the first words out of his mouth were "What the *fuck?*"

His initial reaction was to push the motherfucker away from him, but he instantly became aware of the fact that he wasn't in bed—in fact, he was falling out of the sky, he was fully clothed in combat gear, *and* the motherfucker in question was none other than his teammate Izzy Zanella, who'd hooked Tony into his own oxygen bottle, no doubt to save Tony's life.

There was noise over his radio headset—the CO and the chief both calling his name—and as he and Izzy tumbled and turned, Tony caught a glimpse of a stack of HAHO canopies way, way up in the sky.

He had no idea how he'd gotten here—but logic dictated that at some point in the recent past he'd jumped out of a plane, and evidently hijinks had ensued. Something had gone rather radically wrong. The details of that wrongness, however, could wait.

Years of training kicked in as Tony grabbed more tightly onto Zanella—who was out cold—even as he checked his altimeter, and announced to the team, "I'm okay, but need info. Hot zone or safe?"

He had no idea where they were. Was that desert they were falling toward in California or somewhere else entirely? Afghanistan or some other sandy, desolate, dangerous place...? The mountains in the distance didn't look like A-stan's craggy peaks, but there were parts of that country he hadn't yet explored.

"Safe, repeat you are safe. And I'm right behind you." Chief Lopez's voice was calm and even as it came through Tony's headset—as if they were taking a stroll on the beach instead of falling out of the sky at a hundred-plus miles an hour.

Tony did a quick inventory and saw immediately that his main chute was gone—he'd cut away from his HAHO canopy. Or maybe Zanella had cut away for him. Either way, their in-one-piece arrival on the ground was now up to his reserve chute, which was set to pop automatically when he reached twenty-five-hundred feet.

Izzy's own AAD or automatic activation device was no doubt set to pop *his* reserve, too, and the last thing either of them needed was for their two chutes to tangle and leave them with none. *Two is one and one is none* was an old SEAL adage, but this case was an exception.

The options were a) to keep one of the reserves from engaging its auto-open, or b) to separate from Izzy and let nature take its course.

But if Izzy wasn't breathing, doing that could have deadly results.

The chief was on the same page. "You'll be low enough soon, Vlachic. Pull Zanella's mask, and set reserves to manual."

"Already done, Chief."

"You'll hit the ground before me," Lopez told him. "I'll try to open lower so I'm right behind you, but remember, the added weight will bring you in hard and fast."

Tony knew that, glancing again at his altimeter. "I'm ready," he said.

"Go!" Lopez ordered, and Tony popped his reserve chute and clung like a bastard to Izzy.

He would not let go. He would *not* let go.

"Reserve chute is open," Lopez's voice reassured him through his headset, "and looking good."

In Tony's arms, Izzy coughed and then retched and then, yes, threw up down the fronts of both of their uniforms.

Another reason Chief Lopez had wanted that mask off—hypoxia usually made Zanella hurl. Part of the SEALs' training was to take a class in which they experienced the intense effects of hypoxia—in order to learn to identify it quickly when it happened. And since symptoms changed with age or with weight gain or loss, it was a class they all took a little too regularly.

"Ah, fuck," Izzy mumbled as they drifted to the earth. "Sorry, man…"

"I knew it was coming," Tony told the teammate who'd saved his life. "In fact, I hoped it was coming."

"Then, by all means, *You're welcome*," Izzy said in between his attempts to suck in air.

"Heads up, Vlachic," the chief's voice sharpened. "Pay attention—"

"I am," Tony cut him off. "I got it." SEALs practiced for this, too, and he braced for the larger than normal jolt—kind of like jumping down a flight of stairs with a two hundred pound pack on his back. His knees were gonna feel this, no doubt about it.

But he threw himself into a kind of an awkward run as they landed, letting the motion push him forward instead of resisting and trying to stick the dismount. It was fugly, but it worked, and he and Izzy ended up in a tangle on the rocky desert ground with a relatively small amount of scrapes and bruises.

"Fuck!" Tony heard Chief Lopez utter a rare-for-him obscenity, followed by several strongly worded statements in Spanish.

"No," Tony assured the chief as he released the reserve chute, ensuring that a gust of wind wouldn't drag them any farther. "We're okay. Repeat, we're okay." He and Izzy just lay there for a moment, catching their breath, vomit covered, but fantastically, gloriously alive.

"Fuck," Lopez breathed again, more quietly this time as he crawled toward Tony and Izzy.

In fact, if Tony hadn't still been connected to Izzy via a collection of bungee cords, he would've gone to assist the chief, who was clearly dragging his right leg behind him.

"Portable hyperbaric tanks are on their way," Lopez said as he helped them unhook from one another.

"And the pizza?" Izzy asked, still lying on his back. He turned his head to look at Tony. "I ordered us a coupla pizzas, too. Extra cheese. We might want to shower first, though." But then he noticed Lopez wince. "You okay, bro? *Chief?*" He laughed. "Gotta get used to that."

The chief smiled tightly at them both. "I was a little too focused on your landing instead of mine."

Izzy pushed himself up slightly, narrowing his eyes. "Ankle or knee?" he asked.

"Knee," Lopez admitted. "But I'll be all right. As far as potential injuries go, this is minor."

Izzy nodded, but it was clear he didn't believe Lopez. Tony didn't either—the man was obviously hurt. But everyone handled pain in their own way, and he knew that what Jay Lopez needed right now was for them to co-sign his bullshit.

Again, they all just lay there for a moment, looking up at the sky. Tony could just barely make out the stack of HAHO canopies—the other SEALs—floating into view.

"So what the hell happened?" he asked, and as the words came out of his mouth, he knew the answer. There was only one good reason he'd be hooked into Izzy's O2.

"Your oxygen failed," Izzy said, adding, "No biggie."

More bullshit to tie up with a neat bow. But okay. The *no biggie* route was exactly how he himself would've reported this incident to Adam, early on in their relationship.

But Adam had made it clear, also early on, that *no biggie* would not fly.

"I hope," Izzy mused, as Tony sat up and started peeling off his soiled uniform shirt, "they bring beer with that pizza, because the inside of my mouth tastes like ass."

"Pizza *after* hyperbaric decompression," Lopez reminded him, and then sat up, too, as the chatter from a distant but approaching helo got gradually louder. He dug for a bottle of water and handed it to Izzy, who used the first spray to rinse and spit before passing it on to Tony.

"A man can dream," Izzy said, then broke into song. "*Sometimes, all I need is a pizza to eat!*" He laughed. "Sorry. Song's stuck in my head. Pizza is, too, but pizza generally takes up a lotta real estate when I'm this hungry, post breakfast-giveback."

Tony laughed as he handed the water bottle back to Izzy. But when the big SEAL reached for it, Tony hung on, forcing eye contact.

"Seriously," Tony said. "How bad was it?"

Izzy just shook his head—it was clear he was sticking with his *no biggie* reality. It was the Chief who quietly said, "You and Adam might want to consider naming your firstborn *Irving*."

"God, no," Izzy said, recoiling. "Not only is that child abuse— and trust me, I know. But we're even. I helped you, you helped me. And here we are. On the ground and unharmed. That's how this works."

But Tony persisted. "If my oxygen really did fail at thirty thousand feet—"

"Not *if*, bro," Izzy pointed out. "It failed. Really. But the system didn't. The system worked." He smiled, then, but he stayed dead serious for a change. "That's what we tell Eden and Adam," he continued. "Right? Not *Whoops, we almost died so everyone freak the fuck out,* but *Good news, sweetheart, the system works.*" He went on as if he were Tony talking to Adam, even going so far as to mimic Tony's slightly lower voice, "*Hey, babe, yeah, so my equipment malfunctioned, but my teammates' quick thinking along with their expert-level skill from years of training turned a dangerous situation into a technical problem that was safely solved.* Boom. This *could* have been catastrophic. But it wasn't because..." He held out his hands in a gesture that was half *tah-dah* and half gracious acceptance of imaginary applause. "SEALs. *It's actually a good thing, today's malfunction, because it's proof that despite the danger, we can handle anything that's thrown at us.*"

Tony nodded, but then shook his head. "That last bit? *A good thing?*"

"Yeah, I heard that coming out of my mouth," Izzy said, raising his voice to be heard over the approaching helo, "and I also thought, *nope.* I say *good thing* about anything like this and Eden's gonna start narrowing her eyes. The message is *We're good at what we do and we're not alone.* SEAL *team.* That means something. And she knows it. Adam does, too."

Tony nodded again. "He worries. A lot."

"Best we can do," Izzy said, "is just keep coming home." He then held up his hand in a Vulcan salute, from Star Trek. "*I have been, and ever shall be, your friend...*"

Tony must've looked surprised or maybe confused, because Izzy immediately explained, "The portable hyperbaric chamber looks like that white pod from Star Trek II, you know, Spock's coffin, only it went down to the Genesis planet so he was reborn and—"

"I know my Trek," Tony cut him off. "But *that's* what Adam needs to hear. Yeah, we're good at what we do, and SEAL *team,* you're right, but..." He looked from Izzy to Jay Lopez and back, "Bottom line is that I'm lucky as hell to have friends like you."

CHAPTER NINE

Ben didn't have a concussion, thank the Lord.

And the SEAL team—including Izzy, Danny, and Adam's Tony—had returned to Coronado, but not without mishap.

Jay Lopez had apparently landed wrong, and really messed up his knee.

Plus, there had been some *glitch* that had put both Tony and Izzy into hyperbaric chambers. Allegedly "as a precaution."

Eden had stepped away from the latest round of wine tasting to take Adam's call out on the winery's porch. He'd been diligently texting with reports about both Ben and the HAHO jump, but now he said the words she'd been waiting to hear: "Tony and Izzy are fine. I'm looking at them both right now. They're in my living room. Danny, too." And then he said the words that convinced her that her husband truly was okay: "Izzy's gonna call you in a second—because he knows I'm on with you, he's ordering a pizza first."

"Oh, thank God," Eden said on an exhale. She looked up to see that Jenn had followed her outside. "They're okay. Danny, too." She asked Adam, "How's Jay?"

"Chief Lopez is getting X-rays and, I don't know, maybe an MRI?" Adam reported. "He's pretending his knee's okay, but... I dunno. Mark Jenkins is with him. Danny and Izzy came here to pick up Ben and—"

His voice cut off as Izzy, no doubt, took his phone. Because there was Izzy's familiar, warm voice suddenly in Eden's ear. "Hey, sweetheart."

"Izzy," she said. "Hi," and Jenn faded back inside to give her privacy.

"How's Napa?" he asked.

"Beautiful and delicious," she told him. "Jenni and I are only tasting vinegar and olive oil, and, you know, grape juice—" She cut herself off. "You're really okay?"

"I am," he said. "But."

"Uh-oh."

"Yeah," he said. "There was a mishap. Tony's oxygen malfunctioned, but we figured it out and got him to the ground safely."

Eden wasn't fooled by his use of the plural *we* and she sat down on a bench because her knees were suddenly weak. "But just you and Tony went into the tank thing. Although Jay Lopez was the one whose knee got hurt... "

"He landed wrong," Izzy explained. "He was following us— faster than the other guys, who were still in the HAHO stack—in case we needed medical attention."

"*We* being you and Tony," she clarified.

"Yeah," Izzy said. "I was in the best position to help Tony when his O2 failed, so I did." He then went into detail, telling her exactly what had happened, what he'd done, and what Tony had ultimately done.

Dear God. Eden was glad she was sitting down. "On the danger scale of one to ten—" she started.

Izzy didn't hesitate. "Two," he said. "The situation was not a walk in the park, but... Well, think of it like this, Eed. Tony needed help, and I went to help him first—and it got done. If it hadn't, then Danny would've gone to help Tony *and* me. And if Danny had failed, then Jenk or the CO or even Ferd the FNG would've done it. But we didn't get that far. We didn't need to. Right?"

Eden felt herself nodding. "Right," she said. "Good. Thank you for being honest with me."

"Always," he promised.

"Is Adam freaking out?" she asked.

"Adam is..." Izzy paused. "Ah, they went out in the back yard to talk and... No freaking, at least not visible from the window. *And* big Hollywood kiss. *Some*one's having *I came closer than usual to dying today* sex tonight, and sadly it's not me."

Eden laughed and said the words she knew Adam was saying, right now, to Tony, out in their flower-filled back yard. "I love you." She added, "I'll be home tomorrow night."

"And I," Izzy said, "will be right here, waiting for you."

Provided he didn't deploy...

But that was like the Navy SEAL version of adding "in bed" to every Chinese cookie fortune. You will meet a tall, handsome stranger... *in bed.* Your luck is about to change... *in bed.* I'll be right here, waiting for you... *provided I don't deploy.* We'll be

having a wonderful anniversary party with all of our friends...
provided he doesn't deploy.

It was part of being married to a Navy SEAL. Of course, as Izzy
had pointed out, another part of being married to a Navy SEAL
meant there were dozens of highly skilled and relentlessly trained
teammates always ready to dive out of the sky to protect her
husband.

"Don't let Danny be too rough on Ben tonight," she warned
Izzy. "Adam told me the fight was started by some ass-hat who was
bullying some younger boys. Ben stepped in. And I know, he
should've gone for help, but..."

"He's a Gillman," Izzy finished for her. "The Force is strong in
that one. I don't think we need to worry about Dan getting on Ben's
case about this. Not tonight anyway. We're just gonna make some
dinner, chill, maybe glom a little more *Glee*."

"Danny's actually watching *Glee* with you and Ben," Eden
repeated in flat disbelief.

"It was his idea," Izzy told her. "He heard that the show has an
awesome gay character who has a really cool dad, and well, I'm not
sure Ben even likes it, his tastes run more to the Coen Brothers. But
he really loves that Dan put that much thought into it, you know?"

"Yeah," Eden said. "I kinda love that, too."

There was silence then, for just a moment, then Izzy said, "Life
is pretty good today, huh?"

"Pizza arrive?" she asked.

He laughed. "You know me well, my darling. Yeah. Delivery
car just pulled up out front."

"Life *is* good," Eden agreed. "We should see if Jay needs any
help getting around over the next few weeks. Tell him when I get
back, I'll do a grocery run."

"I love you," Izzy told her. "Madly."

"Hug Adam for me, too," she said. "And tell him what you told
me, you know, the whole *If you hadn't saved Tony, Danny
would've. And if Danny couldn't, Mark would've* and so on.
Thinking of it that way helps. A lot."

"I'm pretty sure Tony already told him that," Izzy said. He
pulled away from the phone a bit to say, "Yeah, thanks, bro. I'll pay
you back."

"Danny paid for the pizza?" Eden asked even though she already knew the answer. "You should go. Eat."

"Are you really okay?" he asked.

"I am," she said, because she really was.

And in the same way that Eden trusted him to be honest about the many things that truly mattered, Izzy trusted her. "I'll call you later," he said.

After Eden cut the connection, she sat for a little bit longer on that porch bench, just looking out at the rolling hills of the vineyard that surrounded her. It was almost insanely beautiful there, and life *was* good.

Still, she sent a text to Adam before she went back inside: *I'm here if you want to talk. Anytime. PS it's okay to feel overwhelmed and terrified.*

She sent a text to her little brother, too, using his long-ago childhood nickname: *I love you and I'm proud of you but holy crap, Boo-Boo.*

Since Ben and Adam were in the same room as Izzy and pizza, she didn't expect immediate replies.

But she knew she'd hear from them both, eventually.

Because just as the men in Izzy's SEAL team always had each other's backs in the sea, on the land, and even in free fall at thirty thousand feet, their spouses and families did, too.

HOME FIRE INFERNO
(Burn, Baby, Burn)

Timeline:

This Troubleshooters story takes place
in January 2010,
around two weeks after *Free Fall*,
and about a month before *Ready To Roll.*

CHAPTER ONE
Jenn

Jennilyn Gillman's water broke.

At first she'd thought it was some kind of horrific pregnancy-induced incontinence. For a few short seconds she'd actually been *glad* that she'd gotten out of her sister-in-law Eden's car and was standing at the side of the road.

But she—and Eden, too—were standing there because the car had broken down on a lightly traveled stretch of highway in the butt-ugly desert, north and east of San Diego, far, *far* from civilization.

"Oh, my God," Jenn said as she realized that the pain that had nearly doubled her over was a labor contraction, and that she hadn't just peed her giant maternity underpants.

No, she was going to give birth. Right here. Right now.

"You okay?" Danny's voice echoed bizarrely over her cell phone, as if her Navy SEAL husband had called her from Mars instead of the Philippines. It was twice as strange that the call from his international cell phone had gotten through, when just moments before neither she nor Eden could get either of their phones to work. Even now, Jenn had maybe a half a bar, at the most. And yet Dan's voice, although distant with that odd echo, was clear.

"Yes," Jenn told him, working hard to keep her voice even. Despite her attempt, she sounded raggedly out of breath, still reeling from the shock of that sharp pain. "I'm fine. Cramp."

It wasn't a lie. Labor contractions *were* cramps, of sorts. And she was fine. Or rather, she was going to be fine.

Dan, however, was going to be full-on, steam-out-of-his-ears pissed when he got the news that she'd born his baby daughter in a ditch at the side of Obsidian Springs Road.

He would've been pissed that she'd even agreed to go on this little road trip through the mountains to the tiny desert "resort" town of Obsidian Springs, even if the trip had been completely uneventful and car-trouble-free.

This was their first pregnancy, and Dan was more stressed out about it than Jenn. Not about the having-a-kid part. He was more than okay with that, happily helping to set up their nursery, and even bringing home a collection of adorable stuffed animals in varying shades of pink. No, it was Jenn who was freaked about her lack of experience with infants, and her imminent responsibility for the life of this completely helpless human being that she was about to drop onto the searing hot asphalt.

Danny's issue was all about Jenn's health. This baby they'd made was already ginormous. It was a full-on mystery to both of them exactly how their daughter was going to emerge from Jenn's womb without medical intervention. If it were up to Danny, Jenn would stay in their apartment, feet up, in their bed, twenty-four/seven, until their little girl was born.

So yeah, the fact that Jenn had gone on this road trip with Eden was going to create some noise when Dan found out about it.

But there was one thing of which she was certain. He wasn't going to find out about it from her, not right now, anyway. Nope.

Eden had opened the hood to glare at her car's engine, but when Jenn had squeaked out that *Oh, my God,* she'd glanced up. Now she looked from the expression on Jenn's face to the liquid still splashing on the pavement between her swollen ankles and sensible sneakers, and her eyes widened. "Oh, my *God,*" she echoed in a much higher octave, at a much louder volume. "Seriously?"

Yes, Jenn agreed that this seemed like a bad joke, because there was *no way* this was supposed to be happening. She was only eight months along. First babies were always late and never early—or so everyone had told her, over and over. It was part of the rationale she'd used in order to convince Eden that it was okay that she ride along with her today.

Meanwhile, Dan had heard his sister and was now asking, "Wait, is that Eden?"

"Dan," Jenn managed to gasp, "I gotta…" She started over, forcing her voice to sound less squeezed and stressed. "I'm sorry, Danny, I'll call you back. I love you! Everything's fine!" She cut the connection as Eden came toward her.

Incredulity mixed with the concern on her sister-in-law's face. "*I'm* sorry, but everything's, like, the *opposite* of fine! Why would you tell Danny that? I mean, even without *this* magic—" she gestured to the puddle on the asphalt "—we need a tow truck at the very least."

"His status—the SEAL team's status—is mission ready." That was all Jenn had to say.

Eden nodded, instantly sober. She got it. Her own husband, Izzy Zanella, was also a SEAL. He was one of Dan's teammates, which meant that *Izzy* was currently mission ready, too. The last thing a Navy SEAL needed was to go into a combat situation distracted by problems from back home. It was a hard and fast rule when sending emails or during these rare phone calls. Everything was *always* fine. It had to be.

"Still, this *might* be an exception to the rule," Eden pointed out.

"Childbirth is completely natural," Jenn countered.

"In four billion degree heat?" Eden shot back, gesturing around them to a landscape that looked like the surface of the moon. "With a bottle and a half of water between the two of us...?"

Jenn looked down the empty road, in both directions. Nothing moved. Nothing real, that is. It was unnaturally hot for January, and heat mirages shimmered and danced. "This is California. Some-one'll drive by. We'll flag 'em down."

"No one passed us on this road when we were heading north," Eden dourly pointed out. "The only traffic was down on Route Seventy-Eight, which is at least five miles in that direction."

Which meant that Obsidian Springs, with its single still-open gas station, was five miles back in the *other* direction.

"Well, they say you're supposed to walk while in labor...?" But not even Jenn could manage to sound optimistic about a five mile hike in this heat.

"Yeah," Eden said. "To *make* the baby come *faster*. I don't think that's what we want here."

"Maybe this was just a freak thing," Jenn said. "I know the fact that my water broke is not good and I need to get to a hospital relatively soon, but there was only just that one contraction—" As she said it, her body proved her to be a liar, another pain hitting her so hard that she had to sit down, right there in the dusty road.

"Come on." Eden looped Jenn's arm around her neck, and lifted the larger woman up. "Let's start by getting you back into the car and out of the sun."

"Oh, my God," Jenn gasped again. She knew from experience that Eden was much stronger and tougher than she looked, with her skinny jeans, her clingy pink top, and her high-heeled sandals.

Eden had, after all, just identified the body of Greg Fortune, her wicked stepfather, at the Obsidian Springs morgue. What the man had been doing in the ghost-town-ish "resort" was unclear, but he'd had a massive heart attack while watching porn on pay-per-view at the Lantern Inn Motor Lodge.

Eden hadn't flinched as the woman in the white lab coat had pulled back the sheet to reveal her stepfather's mottled face. She'd just quietly nodded and signed the paperwork. She'd even settled up his motel bill—which was more than Jenn would've done, had their roles been reversed.

"I love you dearly," Eden told her now as she checked both her and Jenn's phones for a signal, "but I am *not* delivering your baby all alone in the back of my car, in the middle of nowhere. How *did* Danny's call come through? I've tried calling Tracy, I've tried calling Jay, I've tried calling Ben—" all of whom were in San Diego "—I've tried the county sheriff in Obsidian Springs, I just tried nine-one-one, but I get nothing. Even my texts won't send. Maybe an overseas call uses a different cell tower or satellite...?"

"No! I love you dearly, too," Jenn said, reaching out to grab Eden's arm, her fingers tightening as yet another contraction ripped through her—God, that last one hadn't even ended and a new one was starting. It didn't seem fair. She tried to talk through it, and her words came out half-shout, half-snarl, "but you are *not* calling Dan. Or Izzy. They are. Mission. *Ready!*"

Eden gazed back at Jenn with those movie-star gorgeous dark brown eyes that were so like Dan's—except for the fact that she was remarkably unperturbed by Jenn's outburst. It was possible that with everything Eden had been through in her short life, she was incapable of being frightened by anything or anyone.

She was, after all, married to Izzy Zanella.

"I'm not calling either of them," she informed Jenn matter-of-factly as she finished dialing a number and brought her phone up to her ear. "I'm trying the senior chief. Maybe *he* can call Jay Lopez, who can then call Obsidian Springs to get you an ambulance to the nearest hospital."

Where was *the nearest hospital,* Jenn wanted to ask, but as the contraction gripped her harder, all she could do was moan, "Don't let him tell Dan! I'm gonna be fine!"

CHAPTER TWO
Izzy

"I'm having your baby!" Navy SEAL Izzy Zanella sang in his best falsetto. *"I'm a woman in love, and I love what it's doing to me!"*

Dan and Jenk were both on their burner cell phones, talking to their wives—both of whom were pregnant. Mark Jenkins gave Izzy a rueful eye-roll before turning away. Danny just completely ignored him, instead frowning down at his phone as if he'd maybe lost his connection.

And although Danny's wife, Jenn, was farther along in her baby making journey, it was Marky-Mark's wife, Lindsey, who was the biggest cause for concern. She'd miscarried last year, and was playing this current pregnancy super-safe, at least while still in her first trimester.

And yeah, the fact that words like *trimester* were front and center in Izzy's working vocabulary was proof that conversations with both Danny and Jenk had become rather narrowly focused of late.

Izzy knew that Jenn's biggest issue was back aches and swollen ankles, while Lindsey was still actively riding the morning sickness train. Like it or not, he and his other SEAL teammates were getting a crash course in Pregnant Wife 101.

Most of it was not new to Iz, who'd been the youngest in his family. He'd grown up with a pack of much older brothers who'd regularly knocked up their girlfriends and/or wives. Starting in his tweens, there was nearly always someone pregnant in the house, sifting through his fridge, searching for the pickles to top her mint chocolate chip ice cream.

It was essential, always, to have salt-free soda crackers at hand. And the sympathetic words, *I know you feel exhausted/nauseous/awful/homicidal, I'm so sorry, baby, how can I help?* were also good to keep near the tip of one's baby-making tongue.

But both crackers and placating words—along with other gifts like take-out for dinner, or voluntarily vacuuming the house or folding the laundry—were impossible to provide from the other side of the vast Pacific Ocean.

Right now Izzy and Danny and Jenk were sitting in the airport in Manila, moments from being given the *go* to participate in the takedown of a commercial cargo vessel that had been hijacked by pirates from a tiny, neighboring island nation.

Alleged pirates. Rumblings from the intel community had made Izzy rather certain that the nameless tiny island nation's current ass-hat dictator was only *calling* them pirates, and claiming that the cargo ship had been hijacked so as to bring down the full wrath of the US Navy onto their heads. Other rumblings implied that said pirates were, in fact, representatives from the opposition party, meeting illegally to discuss an impending election that would move the country toward democracy.

Another quirky thing about this sitch was that the SEALs hadn't been briefed for this mission in some covert ready room at the nearby US military base. In fact, they'd barely been briefed at all.

Instead, Izzy's team of SEALs, led by the very stern and scary looking Lieutenant Commander Jazz Jacquette, had trooped through Manila's commercial airport in full battle-gear—sans only their weaponry. Which, had they'd been wearing, would've been rattling loudly—sabers and HKs alike. The only thing missing from their ultra-dramatic public display of force had been a neon sign flashing red, white and blue, reading *US Navy SEALs*, while it pointed directly at them in all of their military tough-guy glory.

Izzy was pretty damn certain that his SEAL team wasn't going anywhere—that that *go* command wasn't coming—at least not today. He and his SEAL brothers were, instead, an exclamation point on whatever diplomacy was happening. They were the unspoken *or else* in a message about democracy that was no doubt being delivered to Dictator Ass-Hat.

It wouldn't surprise him one bit if they marched through the airport a few more times before the stand-down order came through, sometime after midnight tonight.

HoboMofo, who was sitting beside Izzy, was thinking the same thing. "I missed Bree's meet-my-dad day at school for *this*?"

The fact that a SEAL who'd been given the most awesome nickname of not just *Mofo*, but *HoboMofo* was the single dad of a girl in the fifth grade was pretty mindbending. Izzy didn't know 'Fo all that well, but if he'd been playing a round of *Two Truths and a Lie* with the other SEAL, and the three statements about the guy had been 1) Wrestles lions for fun; 2) Born on the dark side of the moon; and 3) Lives with his mom and his ten-year-old ballet-dancing daughter named Brianna... Well, Izzy would've picked number three as the blatant, flat-out, had-to-be lie.

Mohf could be best described by someone saying, *Picture the scariest serial killer you can imagine, with a build like a no-neck monster with hams for hands, give him dead, soulless eyes, a buzz-cut that makes his blond hair look oddly colorless and even gray, and then make him twice as huge-large and terrifying... Bingo!*

The SEAL even had the requisite bodies-buried-in-the-back-forty Louisiana bayou drawl.

It was kinda fun imagining him in a "World's Best Daddy" apron, cooking pancakes with mouse ears and dancing with his kid to the soundtrack from *The Little Mermaid. Unda dah sea...* Yeah, that worked for Izzy in a dangerously perfect way. But he swallowed his laughter, because Mohf was clearly bumming at missing his daughter's whatever-it-was at school.

"Didn't I hear you tell Jenkie that Lopez was gonna fill in for you?" Izzy asked. Their teammate, Jay Lopez, had been Left Behind for this current op, after fucking up his knee during a HAHO training jump. He was still hobbling around on crutches, wearing one of those really stupid knee braces that made it so you couldn't bend your leg. But he'd hobble his way into little Brianna's class and flash his perfect smile, and give his super-special G-rated *I am a Navy SEAL* talk.

Most of the little boys and some of the girls in the class would want to grow up to be him. The rest would want to marry him.

Izzy tried to imagine Mohf speaking publicly, even to a bunch of kids, and got a searing vision of sweat pouring off the big man as he attempted to explain the duties of an E-7 SEAL without mentioning the importance of delivering double pops to a terrorist's head to absofuckinglutely make sure they were not just dead, but motherfucking dead.

Yeah.

But whatever Mohf was thinking, it wasn't *Thank you Jesus and Jay Lopez, for saving me from that travesty*. In fact, at the mention of Lopez's name, Mohf shook his head and laughed the way a man might laugh when finding out that his house's sewage line had backed up into the bathtub.

"Yeah," Mohf said, shooting Izzy a decidedly dark look. "Great. That was actually Jenkin's idea. Lopez. *Fuck.*"

Lopez. Fuck. The words didn't make all that much sense. On top of being charismatic and handsome, Lopez was, like HoboMofo, a hospital corpsman—the Navy's version of a medic. He was hands-down *the* nicest guy Izzy had ever met, not just in the Teams, but in the entire US Navy. He was sincerely, honestly kind. His name, Jay, was even short for Jesus.

He was great with kids, women fainted when they met him and...

Oh.

There it was. The reason for HoboMofo's heartfelt *Lopez. Fuck.*

"So how's the school year going?" Izzy asked, trying to sound conversational. "For Brianna. Everything okay? She like her teacher... Missus... or maybe *Miz...?*"

Hobe was a SEAL, which meant that, even as scary and gene-deficient as he looked, he was far from an idiot. He knew exactly what was being fished for, and he gave Izzy his famous dead-eye look. "Yeah," he drawled as he pushed his massive frame up and out of his seat. "She likes her teacher just fine."

As HoboMofo walked away, Izzy reached for his phone. He could at least leave a message for Lopez. *Back slowly away from the hot fifth grade teacher...*

But before he could dial, Danny Gillman plopped his lanky frame into 'Fo's still-warm seat.

"I need you to call Eden," his teammate, former best-frenemy, and still relatively new brother-in-law through Izzy's marriage to Dan's little sister announced. "Something weird is up with Jenn."

CHAPTER THREE
Lopez

Jay Lopez was having a bad week. His injured knee had forced him to remain in San Diego while the rest of his SEAL team went wheels up.

He worked hard to keep the word *hate* out of his vocabulary, but he had to admit that he vehemently disliked being left behind at times like these. And it didn't help his mood this morning when the doctor told him he'd need to keep this brace in place for a few more days, after which *We'll see*. In the medical world, *We'll see* was code for *Yep, you're going to need surgery*, which was disheartening to say the least.

So when Jay walked into the fifth grade classroom of the daughter of the SEAL known as HoboMofo, and was greeted by a teacher who could've played an elf princess in *LOTR*, he was ready for his luck to change.

"You must be Chief Lopez," she said, with a warm, wide grin that worked astonishingly well with her elfin features. Pointy chin, freckle-adorned nose, hazel eyes with long, dark lashes… She was alone in a brightly decorated room that was filled with desks.

His first thought was that he was going to be in town for quite a while—a month and a half, maybe two. Surgery, recovery, physical therapy… It was the perfect time to begin a relationship.

"I am," he told the pretty teacher with his warmest smile, balancing on his crutches so he could hold out his hand to shake. "Although the uniform is probably a pretty large clue."

Her eyes sparkled. "I'm Carol Redmond." Her hand was cool and slender, with short-trimmed nails, and just like that, with that otherwise unremarkable skin-to-skin connection, Jay fell completely in love. "Thank you so much for filling in for Hugh today. I can't tell you how much it means to Brianna to have you here to talk about her dad's work. What can I get you? Would you like to sit down? Hugh told me you blew out your knee—that sounds terrible."

Jay winced. It *did* sound terrible, when put in those words. Especially since a blown-out knee generally required surgery. "No, I'm okay, thanks. It's easier to stay standing." His big question, however, had to do with all of those *Hugh*s.

The puzzlement must've shown on his face, because she laughed again, even as she gently pulled her hand free. "Hugh told me he had a rather complicated Navy SEAL nickname." Her eyes actually danced. "But for some reason, he wouldn't tell me what it is."

"Bert," Jay managed. "I'm sorry, but his name is Bert Bickles." Wasn't it? "I *am* in the right place, aren't I?"

"You are. His full name is Hubert," she corrected him. "He told me he prefers *Hugh*."

"I didn't know that," Jay admitted. "I mean, I haven't worked with him all that much. And even then, we mostly call him..." He stopped himself.

But now Carol's eyes were lit up in anticipation.

"He really didn't tell you?" Jay asked.

"He's a little shy," the teacher said.

Shy? Mohf? *Shy*. Huh. "And you couldn't get it out of Brianna?"

Carol shook her head. "I'm pretty sure she doesn't know. When I asked, she said she thought it had something to do with... Motown?"

Jay laughed. "That's, um... correct."

The elf princess didn't buy it. But she looked around to make sure the coast was clear, and lowered her voice before leaning in to ask, "Mo*fo*?"

Jay lifted both hands in surrender. "You've seen him. You really want me to risk his wrath?"

Her smile was genuinely amused. "He's a marshmallow."

"Yeah, now I *know* I'm in the wrong classroom."

The very lovely Carol Redmond once again laughed, but then a bell rang. "You ready for this?" she asked. "They're coming in from gym, so there'll be a lot of extra energy, combined with the fact that it's the very end of the day. If you want, I can give 'em a spelling test, or maybe a pop quiz on this morning's math lesson. That'll put 'em in a stupor..."

She was kidding. "I got this," Jay said.

"I believe that you do." Her smile was warm and held promises of many wonderful candlelit dinners over the next few months.

Jay felt his phone buzz as a text message came in, but he ignored it—preferring to smile back into Carol's eyes as the first wave of fifth graders came storming into the room.

CHAPTER FOUR
Izzy

Something weird was up with Jenn.

Or at least that was what Danny had just stated as an irrevocable truth. Dude believed it, too. While his body language was all slouchy and playing-it-cool as he sat beside Izzy in the hard plastic airport chairs, Dan couldn't disguise the fact that he was wearing his trying-not-to-freak face.

Izzy sighed, because, Jesus. Jenn's ninth and please-god-final month of baby-cooking was going to be one long, trying endurance test for all of them.

Danny being Danny, Izzy's tiny little barely-there exhale pissed him off. "Look, I was talking to her," Dan said, heavy on the affronted. "And something was definitely up. She just suddenly had to go. And she hasn't called me back."

"Maybe she had to pee," Izzy suggested, while across the waiting area Senior Chief Wolchonok turned to scan the group of SEALs as if he were counting heads. His patience was much like that of a kindergarten teacher or a den mother, only he was far more world-weary and grim. He saw that Izzy was looking at him and as their eyes met, Izzy realized the senior was holding his phone to his ear.

Izzy was just about to leap to his feet and say, *You need sump'n, Senior...?* But Wolchonok's gaze shifted to Gillman, and then back, and then the man shook his head, just a little, like a pitcher shaking off a signal from his catcher. Hmmm. So instead, Izzy kept his convo with Dan-bo going—what were they talking about? Ah, yes. Urination. "Pregnant women frequently have to—"

"She would've told me." Dan cut him off, completely oblivious to Izzy's and the senior's little charades game. "*I have to pee.* Or she would've just taken her phone with her into the bathroom."

"Maybe it was number two," Izzy said as he watched the senior chief pull the phone from his ear and gave it his best death glare, after which he pointed at Mark Jenkins and made a *come here* gesture. Jenk snapped to it. "Women can definitely be all private and weird about doing number two while on the phone and—"

"I'm pretty sure she's with Eden," Dan interrupted again. "First Jenn goes *Oh my God*, and then someone else—Eden—goes *Oh my God*, and suddenly Jenn has to hang up."

Yeah, something was definitely up. Across the room, Senior and Marky-Mark Jenkins were in a deep discussion, and now Mark had *his* phone out, too. Right in front of the senior.

Even though they weren't supposed to bring personal cells on a mission, the SEALs nearly almost all did it anyway, carrying international phones with SIM cards—because they subscribed to the Navy SEAL adage *Two is one and one is none.*

As Izzy watched, their XXL CO joined them, and then *he* got his phone out, as well.

But Danny hadn't noticed—he was in his own oblivious, miserable world.

"*Oh my God* is an appropriate exclamation," Izzy pointed out, "for everything from an apocalyptic mega-earthquake to finding an awesome deal on a newborn-size Star Trek uniform onesie. With Ben coming home from school with an A on his latest English paper somewhere in the middle there."

Dan and Eden's younger brother Ben was still in high school. Izzy and Eden shared custody of the kid with Danny and Jenn. It worked out nicely, with Ben bouncing between their two apartments, and Eden, Jenn and Ben hanging together for extra home-fires-burning support when the SEALs were out in the world, doing their sea-air-and-land thang.

"And there has *not* been an earthquake," Izzy quickly continued as he realized he'd put a bad idea into Dan's already too-noisy head. "At least not the Big One. We would've heard about it by now—it'd be all over Twitter. Seriously, bro, what's the absolute worst that this weirdness could be? That Jenn's gone into labor, right? *Oh, my God, I'm having this massively giant Gillbaby, right—aaahhh!— now—uuuhhh!* Well, if that's the case, then good news! *Some*one's with her. It's definitely not Eden, though. I got an email, said she's driving out to the desert today, to some wanna-be resort town called something appropriately silly like Idiot Springs, to check out some potential wedding reception site for Tracy and Deck. And frankly? *I* should be the one yowling about weirdness. Whatever's up with

Jennilyn, at least she's not a bridesmaid for one of your exes."

Long before Izzy had met Eden, he'd briefly collided with the somewhat ditzy but surprisingly tough-as-nails Tracy, who had finally found a forever home with former SEAL chief Larry Decker. They were planning a big wedding, and Tracy had asked Eden to be a bridesmaid.

"That *is* weird," Mark Jenkins agreed, sitting down on the other side of Danny. Somehow he'd made it across the room without Izzy noticing. But, yup. The senior and the CO were still leaning against the far wall, still working their phones. And the tadpole, Tony Vlachic, had just joined them, his phone out, too.

Curiouser and curiouser.

Izzy turned his attention to Mark, who was purposely mimicking Dan's faux-whatever body language. He looked equally loose and relaxed. And barely legal, with his golly-gee freckles, boyish face, compact frame, and lean build. One of these days, dude was gonna Ron-Howard. He'd pull off his hat, be balding underneath, and suddenly look his age. But until that day, probably well into his forties, Mark Jenkins would continue to get carded.

"Senior wants you, Zanella," Mark told Izzy, managing to keep his tenor sounding calm and matter-of-fact. But he opened his eyes, just a millimeter wider, shooting Izzy a message-filled look while Dan's head was down.

Ruh-roh.

Izzy answered with a questioning narrowing of his own eyes, to which Mark responded with a tip of his not-quite-red head, complete with a pointed look at the senior, as if to say, *All your questions will be answered, douchebag, if you simply stand up and cross the room.*

So Izzy stood up and crossed the room, leaving Markie-Mark to distract Danny with some scintillating pregnancy-related topic. "Lindsey's having these crazy erratic swings regarding food," he heard Mark say as if he really gave half a shat. "She gets these cravings, but in the time it takes me to cook dinner, the thing she was craving now completely grosses her out."

"Take her out to eat," Izzy heard Dan recommend. "Or get to-go and order two very different meals. Then be ready to give her yours when the food comes. Switch plates again, halfway through. Works like a charm."

Meanwhile, the muscle was jumping in Senior Chief Wolchonok's very square jaw. In true senior chief manner, he cut through the bullshit and got to the point. "I got a phone call from Eden," the senior said, and Izzy swallowed the surprised urge to say *My Eden?* Because really, it wasn't as if they knew a dozen different Edens. His wife's name was relatively unique.

Instead, as Izzy instantly did the math and realized that Danny was probably right and Eden *was* with Jenn, the senior chief confirmed that.

"She's with Jennilyn Gillman. Her car broke down, they're out of town somewhere in the desert, they're having some kind of weird heat wave, and Jenn's gone into labor."

Izzy turned inappropriate surprised laughter into a cough that didn't fool Wolchonok.

"Before your wife could tell me where they are," the senior grimly continued, "the signal broke up. I haven't been able to resume contact with her. I'm hoping you can help."

"Eden told me she was going out to Obsidian Springs," Izzy said. "But with Tracy, not Jenn. FYI, it's a Palm Springs wanna-be, not far from Borrego Springs, and even less successful." At his words, the rest of the telethon team sprang into action, including the senior. They all started barking orders into their phones.

Izzy got out his own phone, and speed-dialed Eden. "Come on, come on, come on," he said as the thing first searched for a signal, and then went straight to his wife's voice mail.

CHAPTER FIVE
Lopez

"Every member of a SEAL team has a specific job," Jay told the roomful of wide-eyed ten- and eleven-year-olds, and one very attractive twenty-something—after he'd explained to them exactly how he'd gotten injured. He knew they wouldn't be able to focus until he got that story out of the way, and it had eaten into much of his time. He now had maybe twenty minutes left before school ended for the day.

But that was great. He'd leave 'em wanting more—especially the twenty-something.

"Every SEAL has a specific area of expertise," he continued, "in addition to being able to handle explosives, fire weapons, swim, run, jump out of planes—these are skills that all SEALs have, right? But we each also have a few talents that are unique, that we bring to the team, that make the team stronger. And when our COs— commanding officers—and our senior chiefs are deciding who to send on a mission, they take that into account. For example, I'm a hospital corpsman. Who knows what that means?"

Carol Redmond was smiling—*she* clearly knew what it meant. It was, to be honest, Jay's deal-closer. He knew exactly what he looked like. With his dark hair, brown eyes, handsome face, and trim physique, he knew he had the ability to catch a pretty woman's eye. His being a SEAL helped out in that department, too. But women liked men who saved lives, and it was the fact that he was a hospital corpsman that got him the non-hesitating *yes* when he asked a woman out to dinner.

But that was a question for later.

Right now, several hands shot up around the room, but Jay called on HoboMofo's daughter, Brianna, who looked almost shockingly like her gigantic father, with the same thick blond hair and wide blue eyes. With her redwood-tree-like build, Bree already towered over her teacher. Although unlike her dad's angry ogre affect, the girl's default expression was a charming, quicksilver smile that transformed her completely. She was pure strapping milkmaid—with an easy-going manner that was sweet and friendly.

"A hospital corpsman is like a paramedic." Brianna turned to speak to the entire class. "You know, when you call an ambulance, paramedics are the ones who show up and perform first aid and save everyone's life."

"That's right," Jay said. "And why do you think Hobo...*Bert!*" He cleared his throat. "Excuse me, *Hu*bert, Brianna's dad, and I— why do you think we rarely serve together on the same team?"

"Because you're both hospital corpsmen," Brianna answered triumphantly.

"That's right," Jay said, smiling back at the girl, aware that her teacher was watching and smiling, too. Yes, he *was* very good with kids, thanks. "And most seven or eight men SEAL teams need only one. Because they also need a radio man, an explosives expert, a point man—he's the guy who goes first when you go into dark and scary places—that's an important job." He ticked them off on his fingers. "A sniper, a commanding officer—can't forget him, he's in charge." The classroom door open, and an older woman poked her head in. As Jay kept talking, he watched Carol cross toward her. "And depending on the mission, we might need a languages expert, or a computer expert, or a variety of other types of experts."

Brianna raised her hand, and Jay called on her again as, heads together, the two women spoke. "I can think of a op where the CO would want an entire SEAL team of hospital corpsmen," she said. "If there was an earthquake, and a hospital got destroyed...?"

"For humanitarian efforts, yes. Good one." From the corner of his eyes, Jay saw both Carol and the other woman turn and look directly at him.

Something was definitely up. "I'm guessing I shouldn't have set my phone on silent," he said as he balanced on his crutches to pull it out of his pocket. He flicked it on and...

Holy crap. Twenty missed calls, and a whole slew of texts that said... Danny's wife Jenn had gone into labor, *where?*

"I'm sorry," he said, already hobbling his way toward the door. "I have to run."

But the look on little Brianna's face made him realize that he'd frightened her. She'd leapt to the conclusion that if a SEAL with an injured knee was being called in, something terrible had happened to the SEALs—like her father—who were already out in the world.

"Everything's fine," he told her, told the whole class. "But a bunch of my friends are overseas on an op with Bree's dad, and another of my friends is going to have a baby—right now. And I need to go help her, because her car broke down out in the desert, about an hour outside of town."

As the words left his lips, Jay realized that he didn't actually have any way to help Jenn. Because of his knee, he wasn't driving his car. He'd gotten dropped off at the school by his teammate Tony V's fiancé, Adam, who was an actor. Adam was currently filming an indie movie down by the Del, on the beach in Coronado, and he wasn't going to be able to swing by to pick Jay up until after four. At the earliest. Jay's plan had been to hang at the nearby library until Adam returned.

Now, Jay looked at Carol Redmond. "I don't suppose you have a car that I can borrow. Maybe...?" His teammate Izzy Zanella had a song for every occasion, and the irreverent SEAL's voice echoed in Jay's head. *Hey, I just met you. And this is crazy...*

Carol laughed her surprise. "Can you even drive? I mean, with the..." She gestured to his brace.

He nodded. "I'll take it off."

"Won't that hurt?"

Yes, but at least he'd be able to help Jenn. "I'll be fine. I'm sorry to ask, I know you don't really know me, but—"

"No, it's okay." Carol hurried to the big desk positioned at the front of the room, pulling an enormous, slouchy bag from the bottom drawer. She put it over her shoulder as she began sifting through it, hopefully searching for her car keys.

"Brianna's dad, Hugh Bickles, called the office, hoping to reach you," the older woman said. "Apparently there's been a major accident north of Borrego Springs, and all emergency vehicles are tied up."

"Dawn, this is Chief Jay Lopez. Jay, Dawn—Mrs. Breckenridge—is the school principal." Carol threw out a quick introduction as she pulled out her keys. But she clearly was hesitating to just hand them over to Jay, instead looking at the other woman. "I don't have bus duty today," she started.

The principal nodded. "Go ahead. Drive the chief where he needs to go. The bell's going to ring in a few minutes. I've got your class until then."

"Thank you, Mrs. B," Carol said and Jay echoed her.

She led the way out of the room, and broke into a run in the empty corridor. "Follow me out this door," she called, pointing ahead of her. "I'll get the car, pull it around!"

Carol was kind, beautiful, *and* a quick-thinker while under pressure. If Jay hadn't already fallen hard for her, he'd now be total toast.

CHAPTER SIX
Eden

"First time mothers are always late. There's no way this baby's ready to make the scene. Certainly not today." That's what Jenn had told Eden, in order to let her ride shotgun on this mission of misery.

Freakin' Greg. Eden's stepfather was still making life hard for her, even from beyond the grave.

Late last night, when she'd gotten the call from her too-pathetic mother telling her that Greg was dead, Eden's friend Tracy had immediately volunteered to go with. But that was before Tracy had a three a.m. visit from the Food Poisoning Fairy, and spent the wee hours of the morning sharing intimate secrets with her new porcelain BFF. And shortly after *that* was when Jenn proclaimed that she, instead, would keep Eden company, because *always, no way, certainly not today...*

Famous last words, Alex, for three hundred.

"Right about now I'm regretting not letting Ben come with us," Eden said to Jenn as she helped her into the back seat of the car. Her little brother had gone pale at the news of nasty Greg's passing, and yet he'd asked to come along. But only one of the Gillman siblings was needed for this unpleasant task, and since Danny was out of the country with SEAL Team Sixteen, it had fallen on Eden's shoulders.

"Believe me," she'd told Ben when she and Jenn had dropped him at the high school, "if Danny were home, I'd skip this magic show, too."

"I was just thinking *thank God Ben's* not *here*," Jenn admitted, soggy and sweating and out of breath from that contraction.

Truth be told, it was almost as hot inside of the car as it was out on the road. Eden opened up the other two doors, hoping for a cross-breeze that didn't come. She now took inventory of everything in the car's glove compartment and trunk. The only useful items were an old beach blanket and a small bottle of hand sanitizer. And that was going with a very generous definition of the word *useful*.

"I mean, Ben would want to go get help," Jenn continued breathlessly as Eden scanned the road, hoping for an approaching car, but coming up empty. "And then we'd have to worry that he was alone on the side of the road, and that he'd bump into some motorcycle gang of white supremacist survivalist skinheads, except wait. *He* could stay with me while *you* went to get help..." At Eden's look, she added, "Well, obviously, in any fight between you and survivalist skinheads, *you'd* win."

It was nice to know that Jenn had that much faith in her. But as another contraction started and Jenn grabbed hold of Eden's hand and attempted to breathe through it, Eden was hit with a massive wave of overwhelm that she quickly hid.

She knew she could help Jenn deliver this baby, even here in the back of the car. Her sister-in-law was healthy and strong, with nice wide, womanly hips. This baby would probably pop out of her easily—piece of cake. Eden hoped.

But Eden also knew that sometimes babies were born needing immediate medical aid, and she was full-on screaming terrified that this roadside delivery would turn into a horror show, with that baby gasping for air in her arms, God help her. Because there'd be nothing Eden could do to save it.

Her.

This baby was a girl—Jenn and Dan had found that out months ago when they'd had their ultrasound.

Eden let Jenn hang on to one of her hands as she used her other to try dialing her phone again. She'd gotten through to the senior chief once, surely she could do it again. But she couldn't connect and she couldn't connect. So she focused on Jenn and the fact that Senior Chief Wolchonok was a very smart—if slightly scary—man.

Still, if anyone had the brainpower to track them here, it was Izzy. And Eden found herself wishing she'd broken the rule and dialed her husband instead.

CHAPTER SEVEN
Lopez

Jay had the front passenger seat pushed all the way back and reclined, so that he could sit in the front with his knee brace on. As Carol Redmond drove, he worked the GPS on his phone, not only trying to find the most direct road to Obsidian Springs, but attempting to figure out the route that Jenn and Eden might've taken. Luckily, there just weren't that many ways to get there and back, so they weren't going to have to criss-cross the county, searching for the disabled car.

Also, he knew where Eden and Dan's little brother Ben went to school. Odds were good the two women had headed east directly after dropping him that morning. Which meant they'd taken Route 78 for quite a few miles, before heading north on Obsidian Springs Road.

As they barreled east, as the last remnants of the San Diego suburbs fell behind them and the landscape became desolate and harsh, Carol put her little hybrid into warp drive. She was an excellent driver—confident and sure—and clearly unafraid to push the speed limit. She glanced over at Jay, no doubt because she felt him looking at her, and smiled.

"You ever deliver a baby before?" he asked her.

She shook her head as she turned back to the road. "No. You?"

"No," he admitted. "I've stood by—assisted, but…"

"Not a whole lot of opportunities for a Navy SEAL hospital corpsman to practice delivering a baby," she noted.

"Nope," he agreed. "So, it's been a while."

Carol glanced at him again. "You scared?"

Jay laughed at her directness. "A little, yeah. This baby's about a month early. So yes, scared and worried and a little freaked out pretty much covers it."

Carol nodded. "So our plan should be to get her into the car immediately—get us all moving toward the nearest hospital." She paused. "Where *is* the nearest hospital? It'd be good to know that going in."

Jay was already using his phone's GPS to find that information—but it was rough going because they were already in some kind of cellphone hell-zone. "Are you sure you're not secretly a SEAL chief?" he asked.

"Nope," she said. "But I've got a kind of major crush on one, so…"

Oh, be still his wildly pounding heart! "The feeling is quite, *quite* mutual," he said.

"Really? Oh! Oh my God," Carol said, but he didn't get to hear the rest of whatever she was going to tell him, because his phone rang.

Caller ID presented him with a number he didn't recognize, and he answered it hoping whoever was on the other end would have more information as to Jenn and Eden's whereabouts. Coordinates. Coordinates would be nice. "Lopez." He punched the speaker, so Carol could hear, too.

"Chief!" The voice on the other end echoed oddly, but otherwise was clear. "It's Jules Cassidy. Where are you?"

"Heading east on 78," Jay reported, leaning down to scan the sky out both the front and back windshield. "Where are *you*, sir? And please say in a helo soon-to-be over my head."

Jules Cassidy was an upper echelon FBI team leader who had quite a few friends in the SpecWar community. If anyone could get a helicopter on short notice, it was Cassidy.

"Sorry, I'm in DC," Cassidy said. "But I have access to, uh," he cleared his throat "well, let's just say certain communications satellites, and leave it at that. I haven't quite reached Jenn and Eden yet, but I'm working on it. There *is* a helo—a commercial one—headed your way, but we don't have a doctor or even a medic on board."

Jay check his GPS and rattled off their current coordinates. "We're already in the middle of nowhere, still about twenty miles west of the turn off to Obsidian Springs." He shifted in his seat as he scanned the area. "Plenty of room for a helo to land—the only wires are along the state road."

"I'll tell Adam," Cassidy came back. "What color's your car?"

"Blue Honda Civic," Jay reported. "We'll be the ones pulled over, waving our arms." He realized what Cassidy had said.

"*Adam's* in the helo?"

"Yup," Cassidy said. "Someone—Tony probably—got through to him on set, out in Coronado. They were filming some kind of aerial shot, and Adam commandeered the helicopter—hang on." Cassidy was talking on more than one phone at once, and his voice was muffled as he spoke to someone else, probably Adam in the helo.

"Adam's an actor," Jay lowered his voice to explain to Carol. "A movie star, really. He's engaged to be married to one of my teammates, Tony."

"Gay married?" she asked.

"Yeah, well, I guess… But we just call it, you know, *married*."

"Of course," Carol said quickly. "Right. I wasn't… I was just checking to see if maybe I misunderstood and there was a *female* SEAL named Toni in your team, because, frankly, that would be pretty great, too." She pointed in the rear view mirror. "Is that…?"

Jay turned to look out the back. That little dot on the horizon was indeed the helo. It was a larger bird than he expected, and he could tell just from looking that it was capable of moving pretty fast.

"Pull over," he said, but Carol had already signaled and was slowing. "I hate to just abandon you out here," he started, but she cut him off as she put her car into park.

"Nope," she said as they both climbed out of the car. She opened the back to extract his crutches. "Don't worry about me. I'll be fine. Besides, I don't want to leave my car on the side of the road, *and* I don't want to take up any extra space on the helicopter. Also…" She made a face. "I'm kind of a wimp when it comes to flying."

"Uh-oh," Jay said as he tucked his crutches under his arms. "That might be a relationship deal-breaker."

"About that," she said, but the helo was already coming in for a landing. Not only did its huge blades make it impossible to talk, but they kicked up a crapload of dust and dirt.

"I'm kidding," Jay told her as he gently pushed her back into the drivers seat. "Thank you again. I'll call you with an update." His crutches made it impossible to bury his face in the crook of one elbow, so he simply squinted and tried not to breathe in the dust as he hobbled out to where the helo was gently touching down.

Adam slid open the door and was crouched there inside. He took Jay's crutches and helped him up and into the cabin. Jay waved one last time to Carol right before the door slid closed, and they were off.

Adam was shouting something about how Jules—he was on a first name basis with FBI Team Leader Cassidy—still hadn't gotten through to Eden or Jenn, but that the helo pilot was going to follow the road all the way to Obsidian Springs, if necessary.

"Is there a first aid kit on board?" Jay shouted, and Adam pointed toward the back of the cabin.

The medical kit was far from military grade—geared more towards sprains, breaks, burns, and lacerations. It did, however, include a blood pressure cuff, along with tubing and equipment necessary to set up an IV, if one was need. Other than that, if things went south with either Jenn or the baby, Jay would have to improvise.

But he could do this. He *would* do this. Dan was counting on him. He took a deep breath in, and exhaled hard.

It wasn't until then that Jay realized his epic fail. He'd forgotten to get Carol Redmond's phone number. But just as quickly, he realized that wouldn't be a problem.

He could always get her number from HoboMofo. She was, after all, the Mohf's daughter's fifth grade teacher.

The SEAL chief probably had her on his VIP contacts list.

Jay gently pushed the teacher out of his mind as he went to the windows to help Adam and the pilot scan the shoulder of the road for Eden's car.

CHAPTER EIGHT
Eden

A truck went by, but didn't stop.

Eden chased the damn thing, waving her arms and shouting—screaming after it—at the top of her lungs. But whoever was driving was too busy or too frightened to stop.

"*Son* of a bitch!" she said, hands on her knees as she caught her breath. "*Son* of a *bitch!*"

The heat was brain-melting, reflecting up off the road in an oven-worthy wave as she heard Jenn call out for her. "Eden...?"

She ran back to the car. "I'm right here!" she called. "Asshole didn't stop."

"I think... something's... buzzing?" Jenn exhaled hard, which meant she was feeling the start of another contraction. They were coming closer together now, and lasting longer.

Eden held out her hand for Jenn to grab. "Buzzing?" She realized, the moment she said the word, that she'd set her phone to vibrate when they'd gone into the morgue. And she hadn't turned the ringer back on.

Damn it!

Keeping her grasp on Jenn's hand, she reached into the front where she'd put her phone into the plastic cup holder. She touched the screen and... God, there were about fifteen missed calls. All from the same number.

She quickly hit *return call* and put the phone to her ear, but nothing happened. She tried again as Jenn panted the word *shit* from between clenched teeth. Again, nothing.

But then Jenn said, "Uh oh," and Eden looked down to see a tinge of red staining her sister-in-law's maternity skirt. Oh, God! That was *blood*.

"I think that's normal," Eden lied as another contraction gripped Jenn, and she did what she promised Jenn she wouldn't do—she dialed Danny's cell.

CHAPTER NINE
Izzy

Izzy was heading over to where Mark Jenkins was still babysitting Dan when it happened.

He wasn't close enough to hear, but he saw Danny shifting slightly in his seat in order to pull his phone out of his pocket. He saw Dan frown, and read his lips as he said, "That's weird. It's Eden."

Izzy started running as Dan answered and put the phone to his ear.

"Hey, Eden, is everything okay?" Dan said, but then pulled the phone away to look at it as Izzy skidded to a stop in front of him. "Huh. Maybe she butt-dialed me."

CHAPTER TEN
Eden

Eden was incredulous. Jenn had batted the phone out of her hand.

"It was working," she said. "I finally had a connection!" But when she picked it up, it was back to zero bars. "Damn it!"

"I'm fine," Jenn snarled. "*I'm. Fine.*"

"Yeah, you're not," Eden told this woman who, after Izzy, was her very best friend in the entire blessed world. "I was lying about the blood, Jenni. It's not okay, and I no longer give a shit about *mission ready.*"

"But I do."

"I get that," Eden said. "But I need you to think, just for a moment, about the possibility that you're *not* okay. You're *not* fine. And I want you to think about Dan, coming home, and you not being there to meet him."

Jenn was shaking her head.

"This," Eden continued, gesturing toward Jenn, "is now officially a life-and-death emergency. And if, for whatever reason, we can randomly get through to Dan's overseas burner phone out in Wherever-the-hell-he-is, then that's what we're going to do."

It was then that Eden saw it—movement. A car. Way in the distance. Approaching along the shimmering heat of the road.

Except it was moving faster than a car. And it wasn't on the road, it was above it.

"Chopper!" Eden said, but then realized she'd used the Army nickname. "Oh my God, Jenn, it's a helo!"

For some reason, the Navy called helicopters helos, and this helo that was approaching was definitely courtesy of members of the US Navy. Thank you, *thank you*, Senior Chief Wolchonok!

As Jenn pushed herself up to look out the back window, Eden's phone rang. It was that same number—that one that had tried over and over to call her when her phone was stupidly set to silent.

"Thank you so much," she said, uncaring as to who was on the other end. "The helo is here."

"Hey, Eden. It's Jules. Cassidy. I guess Adam and Jay found you. About time you answered your phone, sweetie."

"Jay Lopez is really on that helo?" Eden had to shout above the rapid-fire sound of the blades as it landed in the desert, sending clouds of dust into the air. She quickly closed the car doors on that side, so that Jenn wouldn't choke.

"He is," Jules said, and Eden quickly relayed that to Jenn who nodded forcefully through another contraction, even as Eden put the beach blanket up and around Jenn's head. "We've got both an OB-GYN and a pediatric specialist standing by to assist him, in case that baby doesn't want to wait for you to get to the hospital."

"Thank you, but I need both hands free," Eden said and cut the connection, jamming the phone into her pocket.

Jenn was already pushing herself out of the car, but Eden held her back. "We're gonna carry you to the helo," she told her friend. "Don't want to accidentally dump the baby out onto the desert."

"That would be my preference, too." They both looked up to see Jay. He was wearing his beige chief's working uniform and his usual air of cool, calm confidence and authority.

Eden knew that Jay Lopez hadn't been thrilled when Izzy married her, and she still thought that he didn't like her very much. Whenever he showed up to a party or dinner out with the gang, her heart always sank, just a little, and she tried not to sit too close to him. But right now, she'd never been more glad to see *anyone* in her entire life. "Thank God you're here!" she said.

"Before we get Jenn to the helo," Jay said, "let's see what's going on in the baby zone."

"Oh, *this* isn't awkward at all." Jenn laughed, her sense of humor still intact despite everything. "When we're telling this story to Danny, let's skip this part, okay? We can focus on the helo rescue, and then just have the baby magically appear in my arms."

"You want *me* to look? Would that be less awkward?"

Eden realized that Adam Wyndham, partner to Navy SEAL Tony Vlachic, had gotten off the helo with Jay. He was, oddly enough, dressed only in a bathing suit and flip-flops.

There was a woman behind him—the pilot, come to help carry Jenn since Jay was on crutches.

"She's only dilated a little bit," Eden told them all. "The only way the baby's falling out is if she has some massive contraction while she's walking to the helo. That's why I thought we should carry her. I'd like to get her to the hospital, ASAP."

Jay glanced up at Eden as he caught sight of the blood on Jenni's skirt, and she nodded.

"Let's do this," he said, and Eden thrust both hers and Jenn's handbags into Jay's arms before helping Jenn up and out of the car.

But before they could create a six-armed, three-person sling, a car pulled up and then a truck, and another car.

It was the cavalry, so to speak—friends, co-workers, and family of Izzy's SEAL teammates, all of whom had apparently leaped into action and raced to Eden's and Jenn's rescue when they'd received the senior chief's long-distance distress call.

Kelly Paoletti—a pediatrician, thank God, came racing out of the first car, followed more slowly by Lindsey—Navy SEAL Mark Jenkins's also-pregnant wife—who'd been driving.

Lindsey had to lean against the car for a moment. She didn't so much as have morning sickness as every-moment-of-the-day-and-night sickness, but despite that, Eden wasn't surprised that she'd volunteered to come.

"You okay?" Kelly's husband Tom, who was the former CO of SEAL Team Sixteen and the current head of the private security firm Troubleshooters Inc, had been right behind them in that truck. He stopped to make sure Lindsey, who was one of his top operatives, wasn't going to faint.

"I'm great," Lindsey lied. "It's Jenn who needs help."

But Tom stayed close until Eden's friend Tracy, looking pale from last night's run-in with food poisoning, emerged from the third vehicle along with Eden's brother Ben. Tracy was still moving slowly, so she hung back to make sure Lindsey really was okay while Tom and Ben both ran over to assist Kelly.

But Kelly had already taken command. "Hi, Jenni! Hey, Eden!" she said with her usual good cheer, "Oh, good, Jay, I'm glad you're here. Let's get you into the helo, Jenn, get you to the hospital as quickly as possible, okay?"

Everyone rushed to carry Jenn, and it was easy with so much help.

"Ben, why don't you take my seat on the helo," Adam offered. "I'll stay with Eden's car and wait for the tow truck."

"Thank you so much," Eden told him and all of her friends, as both she and Ben climbed into the helo behind Jenn and Kelly and

Jay.

The pilot got in, the others backed off, the doors slid shut, and just like that they were in the air.

Ben's eyes were wide, his teenage ennui on a temporary hold. "Is Jenni gonna be okay?" he whispered to Eden.

She hugged her brother as they belted themselves in. "Yes," she answered, and for the first time in hours, she truly believed it. "And the baby, too. They both, absolutely, will be okay."

CHAPTER ELEVEN
Izzy

Izzy was sitting next to Dan when the call came in.

He was watching for it—hoping hard it would come soon and be good news. So he caught the sudden movement when Senior Chief Wolchonok straightened up, then looked at his phone, and then brought it to his ear.

The senior was not prone to dramatics. Dude was steadfast, particularly in the face of tragedy—at least when he was on duty. And he was one of those stoically manly men, some years older than Izzy, who considered himself on duty the moment he stepped away from his family and out of his house.

His wife, a former Coast Guard pilot named Teri, had had more than her share of miscarriages as they'd attempted to start a family. She'd nearly died while giving birth, and they'd adopted their second and third kids.

But if Senior was feeling any sort of flashback to the night he'd nearly lost his wife and eldest child, he didn't let it show.

At least not until after that phone call. As Izzy watched, Wolchonok went limp with what could only be relief—just for a fraction of a nano second—before he clenched his fist and made the international gesture for *yes*, complete with three implied exclamation points. Both his relief and that *yes* happened so quickly that if Izzy had blinked, he wouldn't't've seen it.

"Petty Officer Gillman," Wolchonok intoned as he strode across the waiting area toward Danny.

Dan stood up, because you always stood when the senior came at you like that. Izzy and Jenk stood, too, on either side of him. It was clear Dan was clueless, because he shot both of them an *Uh-oh, what did we do now* look.

But Senior held out his hand and said "Congratulations, son," and Dan automatically took it and shook, still confused until Wolchonok added, "You're a father, Dan. Jennilyn and the baby are both healthy and doing fine."

Dan laughed his surprise. "Wait. *What*?"

Lieutenant Commander Jacquette, the team's CO, was right behind the senior chief, and he, too, shook Dan's hand, delivering his congrats in his *basso profundo*. Then the rest of the team surrounded them.

"Jenn had the baby," Dan realized, and he turned to hug Izzy and then Jenkins.

Izzy took the opportunity to sit down. Thank God thank God *thank God*.

But Danny was not an idiot, and he soon realized… "You knew! She went into labor and everyone knew?" He aimed his accusation at the entire team—officer and enlisted alike. Although—again, because he was not an idiot—he waited until both the CO and the senior were well out of range.

Dan turned and punched Izzy in the shoulder.

"Ow! Why do *I* get punched?" Izzy asked.

But Dan was already extracting the details from Jenk, who'd admitted, without any punching, that Jenn had gone into labor while on an impromptu road trip with Eden, because apparently Tracy got food poisoning…?

That didn't make sense, because the whole purpose of the trip was to check out some potential wedding reception site, so why go without the bride-to-be?

Izzy felt his phone rattle in his pants, and he pulled it out to see that Eden had sent him several photos via email. The subject header was *Stealth Penis*.

That was… interesting.

"Callista," Izzy heard Dan say, as he opened the email and the photo slowly uploaded. "Callie, for short. Yeah, no, we picked out that name as soon as we found out we were having a daughter. Holy shit, you guys, I have a *daughter*."

Izzy looked at the first picture—it was a selfie of Eden smiling, her head next to Jenn's. Jenn was in a hospital bed, looking exhausted but happy, with an equally exhausted tiny baby in her arms. The baby was wrapped in a white blanket, with a little blue hat on its head and…

Wait a minute… *Stealth penis*…?

Izzy scrolled to the next shot, which was of Dr. Kelly Paoletti, holding a naked and yowling baby, a big smile on her face. And sure enough...

"Whoa, check out these pictures, Danny," Izzy said. "Eden sent them. Dude! Congratulations! Your daughter has a penis!"

Danny grabbed Izzy's phone and as he looked for himself he started to laugh. "Holy shit, it's a boy. I have a son—with a million pink toys."

"He's a baby, what does he care?" Izzy said.

But Dan stopped on the photo of Jenn in that bed with their baby in her arms, and the expression of gratefulness and love on his face was so private that Izzy turned away.

And found the senior chief heading toward him, on yet another mission. At their eye contact, Senior motioned for Izzy to step away from the crowd.

"Sup, S?" Izzy asked, quickly adding, "and that S stands for Senior not Stan because even though I know that's your name, I'd never call you Stan, Senior."

The senior spoke over him as he handed Izzy a piece of paper. It looked like a short list of airlines, flight numbers, departure times, and gates. The first was a nonstop to Los Angeles. The second went to San Diego, with a stop in Tokyo. The third did the same.

"I just received our stand-down order," Senior told Izzy quietly, "but we won't get a military transport flight out of here until Thursday at the earliest." He pointed to the list. "All of these flights are filled, but these airlines are willing to book passengers on later flights—if you can get anyone to volunteer to give up their seat for Dan."

"Whoa, this first one's boarding in ten minutes," Izzy realized. It was two gates down. He'd made note of the fact, during one of their walks through the airport, that most of the passengers there were American.

This could work.

"I thought maybe you could go over there and quietly see what you could do," the senior said.

"Thank you, Senior Chief."

Senior caught Izzy's arm before he could go. "See if you can't get yourself a seat, too," he said. "Your wife and Jennilyn went up to the morgue in Obsidian Springs to ID the body of her—Eden's—stepfather."

"Oh, God," Izzy said.

"I know you've had trouble with him in the past," the senior continued, "but that couldn't've been easy for her."

Izzy had to agree. "Still, let me get Danny home, first."

Senior smacked him on the same shoulder that Dan had punched, but this time Izzy didn't say *ow*. Especially when the senior said, "You're a good man, Zanella. Get it done."

Izzy went to the gate, and yes, he was right. The passengers here were mostly Americans. He went right to the counter at the front, near the boarding door, and climbed up to stand on top of it.

"May I have your attention please?" he said, using his outdoor voice. "My fellow Americans, my name is Irving Zanella, and I'm a member of your military fighting force. I'm here with about a dozen of my Navy SEAL brothers-in-arms, and one of us, my dear friend Danny, just found that his son—his first child—was born about an hour ago, in a hospital not that far from San Diego. So if anyone here is not in a screaming rush to get back to the States, this very generous airline will put you on a later flight, and let Danny use your seat so he can go home and meet his beautiful, *beautiful* newborn son."

A young woman in the back had stood up when Izzy said the word *born*, and she and what looked like two friends made their way toward him. "We're on vacation," she said. "We'll give you our seats, but we're traveling together, and there're three of us."

Izzy jumped down. "Thank you so much. Three seats would be incredible. Wait here, I'm gonna get my senior chief." He dashed back to where the team was hunkered down.

The senior was shaking his head. "That was quiet?" he asked rhetorically as he went to handle the details with both the volunteers and the airline. Dan went with him, still holding Izzy's phone, no doubt eager to start showing off pictures of his shiny new baby.

Izzy sat down next to Mark Jenkins. "Hey, I know you're in a hurry to get home, too, but would you mind very much if I gave the third seat to Hobe?"

"HoboMofo?" Mark asked, as if there was more than one *Hobe* in the team.

"Yeah," Izzy said. "We accidentally introduced Lopez to his daughter's fifth grade teacher. His daughter's *single* fifth grade teacher, that 'Fo was hoping to get to know a little better…?"

"Aw, shit,!" Mark said. "Yeah, give him the seat, and tell him I'm sorry. *Damn* it."

"Thanks, bro," Izzy said, and went to gather up the 'Fo, who was happy to go home early.

And after they joined Dan at the gate, Izzy took his phone back and emailed his wife.

I love you, he wrote in response to her *Stealth Penis* email. *I'll see you soon. Keep those home fires burning.*

CHAPTER TWELVE
Lopez

Jay was at the hospital when Dan, Izzy, and HoboMofo—the SEAL whose real name was Hugh Bickles—arrived.

They must've rented a car at LAX and driven directly here, after their fourteen hour flight.

Dan came into Jenn's hospital room like a man on fire, and Eden shooed Jay and Ben out into the hallway lobby area, so the two of them—three Gillmans, now—had privacy.

"We have a son," Jay heard Jenn tell Dan. "Are you disappointed? I know you wanted a girl."

"I only wanted a healthy baby," Dan said. "And for you to be okay, too. God, Jenni, I love you so much—"

The door closed on them as Izzy, meanwhile, didn't feel the need for any privacy to soul-kiss his wife. "You okay?" he asked Eden, his hands around her face, their foreheads together.

Eden's eyes welled with tears—it was the first time Jay had seen her come anywhere close to crying. She'd been Jennilyn Gillman's staunchest ally and greatest friend—holding her hand and breathing with her—essentially cheerleading the way throughout what had been an arduous and frightening delivery.

But even now Eden nodded, *yes.* She *was* okay, and clearly very glad Izzy was safely home.

"Daddy!" Jay turned to see Brianna Bickles fling herself into Hobo's—Hugh's—giant arms. The big SEAL lifted up his daughter as if she weighed next to nothing, as he grinned his ass off with a smile that was a lot like his daughter's. It transformed him from angry ogre to... Wow, kinda ruggedly handsome, enormously jacked guy.

Where had Brianna come from? Jay leaned forward in his chair to look down the hall, and sure enough the door opened and there she was.

Carol Redmond.

She'd come out to hospital, apparently giving a ride to Hugh's mom and Bree.

Jay waved to her, but she didn't see him, her smile was aimed at...

Hobo... *Mofo.*

Really?

Really?

Now Hobe was smiling at Carol—and damned if that didn't make him look freaking adorable.

What was it that Carol had told him in the car? That she had a kind of a major crush on a Navy SEAL chief...?

Hubert Bickles, aka HoboMofo, was a Navy SEAL chief.

Wow, *that* would've been really not okay—Jay's hitting on a woman that one of his SEAL brothers liked, or, God, maybe even loved.

What was there *not* to love about Carol Redmond?

Jay felt a pang of regret—a brief little burst of sorrow for what was not-to-be. But it faded quickly as he watched Carol smile up at Hobe—Hugh—her pleasure at seeing him evident in her body language.

"I really wanted to come talk to the class," Hugh was saying, as Briana danced off to join her grandmother. "I'm sorry I had to send a substitute."

"Oh, Chief Lopez was *very* good," Carol told him earnestly. "The kids loved him, he was so sweet with Bree, and then he led me on quite the adventure." She laughed. "It was... educational."

As Jay watched, Hugh winced. "Well, great. That's... great. He's, um, here if you, you know, want to say *hi.*"

He pointed over at Jay.

"Oh, hi, Jay," Carol said as she looked over at him with so much nothing in her eyes, that he almost laughed aloud. She returned her attention to Hubert, even as she moved toward Jay.

He didn't know how she did it, but she managed, without taking Hugh's hand, to pull him with her as she said, "Congratulations. I assume you had something to do with Jenn's and the baby's good health." He was about to stand, but she stopped him. "Oh, no, don't get up."

"I got lucky," Jay admitted. "We have another friend, Dr. Kelly Paoletti—she managed to drive out to where Jenn and Eden were stuck. She took over, so I just assisted, which was fine with me."

"It was the most amazing thing," Carol told Hugh. "After Jay got into the chopper, I decided to keep going. I thought I could help by staying with Eden's car or... I don't know. But when I got there, there were all these people who'd already come to the rescue. Tom and Adam and Lindsey and Tracy. They just dropped everything, because Dan—and you—were overseas."

"That's how it works," Hugh said. "Kinda like Jay filling in for me in a pinch."

"It's so impressive," Carol said. "And you know, if I've seemed at all hesitant, it's because it scared me. The idea of a relationship with someone who's not only got a dangerous job, but who's also always... kind of... gone. But it was great to see how it works. Starting with Jay's amazing generosity and ending with a random group of people all coming to Jenn's rescue—except they weren't random. They're family. They're *more* than family."

Jay could see that Hugh was struggling to understand, and he knew all the big SEAL had heard was "Jay's amazing."

"It really was nice to see that," Carol said again.

"I have an idea," Jay said, because it was so obvious that Hugh was stuck in some terrible parallel universe where he'd returned from the mission to find Jay and Carol already engaged to be married. And unlike that brief pang of regret that Jay had felt when he'd seen Carol smile at Hugh, Hugh's suffering was deep and intense. *Someone* had to put the man out of his misery. "Why don't we go out sometime, like on a double date." He looked at Carol. "You and Hugh, and me and..." He cleared his throat and lied. "Well, there's a woman I've been dying to ask out, and... This'll give me a reason to. Ask her."

"I'd like that," Carol said, looking up at Hugh.

"Um, wow. *Yeah*," he said, light finally dawning. "I'd like that, too. Very much. Thank you." The smile he shot Jay was definitely adorable.

"We could go tonight," Jay said, but then slapped his forehead. "Wait, no, I can't make it, not tonight. But *you* could go. Right?"

"I'm free," Carol told Hugh as Jay found his crutches, and pulled himself up, and slowly backed away.

"Ooh," Hugh said, making an *I don't know* face. "First night back always belongs to Bree."

And it was beyond obvious from the look on Carol's face that those words made her love Hugh all the more.

"We could all go out," she suggested. "Bree and your mom, and... you and me."

"Oh, Jesus, 'Fo," Izzy Zanella said from where he was sitting, his arm around Eden. "Will you just grab her and kiss her already?"

Hugh laughed.

And did just that.

And Carol kissed him back.

Dear Readers,

Free Fall and *Home Fire Inferno (Burn, Baby, Burn!)* are the first two stories in a trilogy of what was supposed to be Troubleshooters shorts. But the third installment, *Ready to Roll,* came in much, *much* longer than a short story. In fact, it's a novella.

It takes place about a month after Jenn and Danny's baby is born—and part of the story returns focus to Ben, who continues to deal with high school bully, Wade O'Keefe.

There's a second interwoven plot line that will introduce you to a new group of young SEAL candidates who are going through Navy SEAL BUD/S training's Hell Week—and their tough-as-nails instructor, LT Peter "Grunge" Greene. Who happens to be a longtime friend of Izzy Zanella.

So yeah. There's plenty of Izzy in the next novella. #ZanellaNovella

Make sure you pick up *Ready to Roll,* because LT Greene also happens to be the hero of my next full-length Troubleshooters book, *Some Kind of Hero,* coming at you in hardcover and ebook from Ballantine Books, and in audio from Blackstone audio in July 2017! (More Zanella in that book, too!)

Watch, too, for the audio editions of *Ready to Roll* and *Home Fire Inferno. Free Fall* is already available as an audio short, read by Patrick Lawlor. You want to hear what Izzy sounds like when he starts making all that noise inside of my head? Check out Patrick's pitch-perfect narration of *Free Fall* or any Izzy-centric story like *Breaking the Rules* or *Into the Storm.* Patrick brings Izzy completely to life!

Last but not least, I'd appreciate it greatly if you'd post a review or toss both *Free Fall* and *Home Fire Inferno* some shiny stars and/or digital buckets o' love at your favorite on-line bookseller. Authors depend on reader reviews more than ever in this crazy, noisy, option-filled digital world. I'm very grateful, too, when you post, share, tweet, text, and talk about my books! (Thank you so very, very much!)

I love getting interactive: Twitter's my social media format of choice—give me a shout @SuzBrockmann. I pop in on my Suzanne BrockmannBooks Facebook page from time to time, too. But if you want to be absolutely certain you'll get hot-off-the-press news about upcoming releases and appearances, sign up for my e-newsletter at www.tinyletter.com/SuzanneBrockmann!

Thank you again for spending your reading time with my characters and me.

Love and hugs,

Suzanne Brockmann

Ready to Roll

Suzanne Brockmann returns to the action-packed world of her bestselling Troubleshooters series with a new novella featuring U.S. Navy SEAL Izzy Zanella, his extended family, and his kickass teammates in SEAL Team Sixteen.

The only easy day is yesterday.
BUD/S (Basic Underwater Demolition/SEAL) training is known for being the toughest, meanest, most physically punishing program in the entire U.S. Navy, and a new crop of tadpoles have arrived in Coronado eager to prove their worth—to make it through Hell Week, and become U.S. Navy SEALs.

Although Izzy prefers assignments out in the "real world," he's happy enough to be TDY as an instructor for the current BUD/S class, because it allows him to spend time at home with his wife, Eden, and her lively and lovable extended family.

Eden's sixteen-year-old brother, Ben, is dealing with a new crush and a homophobic bully in his high school, but it soon appears that things are *not* as they seem.

As Ben deals with the type of too-serious high school drama that could involve a body count, Izzy is intrigued by "Boat Squad John," a misfit team of young SEAL candidates all named John, who include the intriguing young Seagull, his swim buddy Timebomb, and Seagull's nemesis Hans.

Does Seagull have what it takes keep Boat Squad John still standing when the dust of BUD/S Hell Week settles, or will they ring out?

Set in Coronado during BUD/S training Hell Week, in *Ready to Roll* Brockmann introduces the SEAL officer and instructor nicknamed *Grunge*—Lt. Peter Greene—as she delivers what she does best: a story celebrating the U.S. Navy SEALs—and the women (and sometimes men) who wholeheartedly love and support them. *(About 56,000 words or 220 pages)*

Suzanne Brockmann's Navy SEAL Series:

Troubleshooters Series
1. *The Unsung Hero*
2. *The Defiant Hero*
3. *Over the Edge*
4. *Out of Control*
5. *Into the Night*
6. *Gone Too Far*
7. *Flashpoint*
8. *Hot Target*
9. *Breaking Point*
10. *Into the Storm*
11. *Force of Nature*
12. *All Through the Night*
13. *Into the Fire*
14. *Dark of Night*
15. *Hot Pursuit*
16. *Breaking the Rules*
17. *Headed for Trouble* (Short story anthology)
18. *Do or Die*
19. *Some Kind of Hero* (July 2017)

Troubleshooters Short Stories and Novellas
1. *When Tony Met Adam*
2. *Beginnings and Ends (A Jules & Robin Short Story)*
3. *Free Fall*
4. *Home Fire Inferno*
5. *Ready to Roll*

Tall, Dark & Dangerous Series
1. *Prince Joe*
2. *Forever Blue*
3. *Frisco's Kid*
4. *Everyday, Average Jones*
5. *Harvard's Education*
6. *Hawken's Heart (It Came Upon a Midnight Clear)*
7. *The Admiral's Bride*
8. *Identity:Unknown*
9. *Get Lucky*
10. *Taylor's Temptation*
11. *Night Watch (Wild, Wild Wes)*

Fighting Destiny Paranormal Series
0.5 *Shane's Last Stand (e-short prequel)*
1. *Born to Darkness*

Suzanne Brockmann Presents: The California Comedy Series

Suzanne Brockmann Presents a new series of m/m category romance novellas set in Southern California, written by Jason T. Gaffney with Ed Gaffney. Short, spicy, and laugh-out-loud funny, the *California Comedy* series puts the comedy in rom-com. Available in eBook and print.

1. *Creating Clark*
When a handsome actor gives a nerdy friend a Cinderella makeover to help him catch the attention of an attractive man, their lessons in love go a bit too far, putting their longtime friendship at risk.

2. *A Match for Mike*
Sparks fly when estranged childhood friends join forces to rehab a house, but old wounds are reopened, threatening their new romance.

3. *Fixing Frank*
When two reality show contestants learn that their embarrassing past has been discovered by the show's producers, they pretend to be engaged to avoid further humiliation. But when they actually begin to fall for each other, things start to get complicated...
(coming June 20, 2017)

ABOUT THE AUTHOR

After childhood plans to become the captain of a starship didn't pan out, **Suzanne Brockmann** took her fascination with military history, her respect for the men and women who serve, her reverence for diversity, and her love of storytelling, and explored brave new worlds as a *New York Times* bestselling romance author. Over the past twenty years she has written more than fifty novels, including her award-winning Troubleshooters series about Navy SEAL heroes and the women—and sometimes men—who win their hearts. In addition to writing books, Suzanne Brockmann has co-produced several feature-length movies: the award-winning romantic comedy *The Perfect Wedding*, which she co-wrote with her husband, Ed Gaffney, and their son, Jason; and the upcoming thriller *Russian Doll*. She has also co-written two YA novels with her daughter Melanie. Find Suz on Facebook at www.Facebook.com/SuzanneBrockmannBooks, follow her on Twitter @SuzBrockmann, and visit her website at www. SuzanneBrockmann.com to find out more about upcoming releases and appearances.

Made in the USA
Middletown, DE
20 July 2018